The Heir of Two Worlds

By
Arianna Reed

Copyright 2024 Orion Harmony Vale. All rights reserved.

No part of this book may be reproduced in any form or by any electronic or mechanical means including information storage and retrieval systems, without permission in writing from the author. The only exception is by a reviewer, who may quote short excerpts in a review.

Although the author and publisher have made every effort to ensure that the information in this book was correct at press time, the author and publisher do not assume and hereby disclaim any liability to any party for any loss, damage, or disruption caused by errors or omissions, whether such errors or omissions result from negligence, accident, or any other cause.

This publication is designed to provide accurate and authoritative information with regard to the subject matter covered. It is sold with the understanding that the publisher is not engaged in rendering professional services. If legal advice or other expert assistance is required, the services of a competent professional should be sought.

The fact that an organization or website is referred to in this work as a citation and/or a potential source of further information does not mean that the author or the publisher endorses the information the organization or website may provide or recommendations it may make.

Please remember that Internet websites listed in this work may have changed or disappeared between when this work was written and when it is read.

Table of Contents

Chapter 1: A Forbidden Love 1

Chapter 2: Secrets in the Shadows 6

Chapter 3: The Kingdom's Fear 12

Chapter 4: The Witch's Dilemma 18

Chapter 5: A Royal Engagement 25

Chapter 6: Shadows and Pursuit 29

Chapter 7: The Safe Haven 33

Chapter 8: The Child of Prophecy 39

Chapter 9: Whispers of War 45

Chapter 10: The Dark Forest 49

Chapter 11: Lyra's Awakening 56

Chapter 12: A Kingdom in Flames 63

Chapter 13: The Sorcerer's Return 70

Chapter 14: The Prince's Sacrifice 77

Chapter 15: The Coven's Decision 84

Chapter 16: A Fragile Peace 91

Chapter 17: The Gathering of Strength 98

Chapter 18: The Gathering Storm 101
Chapter 19: Lyra's Power 108
Chapter 20: A New Beginning 114

Chapter 1:
A Forbidden Love

The moon hung low over the forest, casting a silvery glow over the trees as Prince Kael rode through the dense woods. His steed moved swiftly beneath him, the only sound in the night the rhythmic clop of hooves against the earth. He wasn't supposed to be here—his father had forbidden anyone from venturing too close to the border, the land where witches were said to dwell. But Kael was no stranger to defying his father's will.

Tonight was different. He could feel it. The cool air prickled his skin, and there was a sense of something watching him, something beyond the usual forest creatures. He tightened his grip on the reins, scanning the shadowed trees for movement.

Suddenly, his horse reared back, startled by a figure that had appeared from the darkness. Kael struggled to regain control, his heart pounding as he dismounted. Standing in the path before him was a woman, cloaked in a deep green robe that shimmered like the forest itself. Her eyes, a striking violet, locked onto his, and Kael felt a jolt run through him.

"Who are you?" he demanded, trying to keep his voice steady.

The woman didn't answer immediately. She stepped closer, her movements graceful and deliberate, as if she were part of the very forest itself. "You're far from home, Prince," she said softly, her voice carrying a melodic quality that was both soothing and unsettling.

Kael's hand instinctively moved to the hilt of his sword, though something in her gaze told him it would be useless. "You know who I am," he said, narrowing his eyes. "Then you must know that you're standing on the king's land. A dangerous place for a witch."

She smiled, though there was no malice in it. "Is that what they call me in your kingdom? A witch?" She tilted her head, the moonlight catching her features, revealing her beauty in sharp contrast to the danger he had always associated with magic. "What would you call me?"

Kael hesitated. Everything he had been taught told him to be wary of magic, to fear the unknown powers it possessed. But standing before her now, there was no fear—only curiosity, and a pull he could not explain. "What are you doing here?" he asked, avoiding her question.

"I could ask you the same," she replied, her gaze unwavering. "Do you always ride so far from the safety of your kingdom at night?"

Kael glanced around, the forest suddenly feeling much smaller than it had moments before. "I... needed air. To clear my mind."

The woman's eyes softened, as if she understood far more than he intended to reveal. "Sometimes, the mind seeks clarity in the most unexpected places."

He frowned, confused by her cryptic words. "And what about you? Why are you here, so close to the border?"

The woman turned slightly, looking up at the sky as if the stars themselves held the answer. "This forest is not part of your kingdom, Prince. It is older than any border drawn by men. I come here often, to be among the trees, to listen to their stories."

Kael shifted uneasily. He had heard tales of witches communing with nature, bending it to their will. But there was something different about her. She didn't feel like a threat—more like a mystery he wanted to solve. "What's your name?" he asked, stepping closer, his curiosity getting the better of him.

She turned her gaze back to him, her violet eyes almost glowing in the dim light. "Elara," she said quietly, and the name seemed to hang in the air between them like a secret shared.

"Elara," Kael repeated, testing the name on his tongue. It felt familiar, though he was certain he had never heard it before. "I've never met a witch before."

Elara smiled again, this time with a touch of sadness. "Perhaps that's for the best."

They stood in silence for a moment, the forest around them eerily quiet, as if waiting for something. Kael's thoughts raced—he should leave, return to the safety of the castle, and forget this ever happened. His father would be furious if he knew Kael was speaking to a witch. But something inside him resisted that instinct. He couldn't walk away.

"Tell me," Kael began, his voice softer now, "why do our people fear you so much?"

Elara's expression darkened slightly, and for a moment, Kael thought she wouldn't answer. But then she sighed, her shoulders lowering. "Fear often comes from ignorance, Prince. Your people fear what they do not understand. And what they cannot control, they seek to destroy."

Kael frowned. He had heard those words before, spoken by his father, but with a different tone. King Ardan had always painted magic as a dangerous, uncontrollable force that threatened the stability of the kingdom. But hearing it now, from Elara's lips, it felt different. It felt... wrong.

"I don't believe you're dangerous," Kael said quietly, almost to himself.

Elara studied him for a long moment, as if trying to decide whether he was worth trusting. "Perhaps you're not like your father after all," she said, her voice barely above a whisper.

The mention of his father snapped Kael back to reality. He took a step back, as if suddenly realizing how close they had become. "I shouldn't be here," he muttered, glancing back at his horse. "I need to go."

Elara nodded, though there was a flicker of something in her eyes—disappointment, perhaps? "Go then, Prince. But remember this night."

Kael mounted his horse, his heart racing. He hesitated one last time, looking back at her. "Will I see you again?"

Elara's lips curved into a mysterious smile. "Perhaps. If the fates allow."

Without another word, Kael urged his horse forward, disappearing into the darkness of the forest. But as he rode away, the memory of her violet eyes lingered in his mind, and he knew that this night was only the beginning.

Chapter 2:
Secrets in the Shadows

Kael couldn't stop thinking about her. Days had passed since his encounter with Elara, but her image haunted his thoughts like an unshakable dream. No matter how hard he tried to focus on his duties, his mind drifted back to the mysterious witch in the forest, her violet eyes lingering in his memories like a flame he couldn't extinguish.

In the grand halls of the castle, he was surrounded by nobility, courtiers, and the constant murmur of palace life. But none of it mattered. The grandeur of his father's kingdom felt hollow, distant. He had grown up learning that his destiny lay in maintaining the power and stability of the throne, yet suddenly, all of it seemed like a cage. It was Elara's voice, her words about fear and ignorance, that echoed louder than the duties he was expected to uphold.

At breakfast, his father, King Ardan, sat at the head of the long table, his face stern and unreadable as always. His deep-set eyes scanned the room, taking in the noblemen and knights who had gathered to discuss matters of the kingdom.

"Kael," the king's voice boomed, pulling him out of his thoughts, "are you paying attention?"

Kael blinked, realizing he had been staring absently at the half-eaten food on his plate. He straightened in his seat. "Yes, Father."

The king narrowed his eyes slightly. "I was speaking of the border patrols. There have been more reports of strange activity near the forests. I want you to lead the next scouting party. You'll take the knights and secure the area."

Kael's stomach tightened at the mention of the border. His last trip there had been anything but ordinary. "Do you really think it's necessary, Father? The witches—"

"The witches are always a threat," King Ardan interrupted, his voice cold. "We cannot afford to be complacent. Their magic is unpredictable, dangerous. It's only a matter of time before they attempt something."

Kael clenched his jaw, resisting the urge to argue. He had seen nothing of the kind in Elara. She had been calm, composed—nothing like the witches his father spoke of with such disdain. "Of course, Father," he said, though the words felt bitter on his tongue.

After the breakfast ended, Kael retreated to the castle's courtyard, trying to find some peace among the quiet gardens. But even here, surrounded by carefully tended flowers and statues of his ancestors, his thoughts were restless. He couldn't stop wondering—what if his father was wrong? What if the witches weren't the threat they had always been made out to be?

"Kael."

He turned to find his sister, Princess **Isla**, approaching him. Her long golden hair, tied in intricate braids, shone in the sunlight as she crossed the garden. Unlike their father, Isla had always been more in tune with Kael's thoughts and emotions. They had grown up close, sharing secrets and ambitions far from the politics of the court.

"You're distracted," she said, tilting her head as she studied him. "More than usual, I mean."

Kael smiled faintly, though it didn't reach his eyes. "It's nothing."

"Really?" Isla raised an eyebrow, her tone teasing. "Because it looks like you've got something—or someone—on your mind."

Kael hesitated. He had never kept secrets from his sister, but this was different. Speaking about Elara felt dangerous, not just because of the fear his father had instilled in him, but because it was something precious, something he wasn't ready to share. "Just the usual," he said, waving his hand dismissively. "Father's plans, the kingdom, patrol duties..."

Isla wasn't fooled. She stepped closer, lowering her voice. "You've been restless for days, ever since you returned from the border. What happened out there?"

Kael looked away, not wanting to meet her gaze. "Nothing important."

"Kael." Her voice was firmer now. "I know you too well. You can't lie to me."

He sighed, rubbing a hand over his face. "You wouldn't believe me if I told you."

Isla's eyes narrowed, curiosity sparking in them. "Try me."

For a long moment, Kael stood in silence, torn between the urge to protect his secret and the need to share it with someone who might understand. Finally, he relented. "I met someone," he said quietly.

Isla blinked in surprise. "Someone? Out there?"

Kael nodded, his gaze distant as he remembered the moment he first saw Elara standing in the moonlight. "A woman. She... she's not like anyone I've ever met. She's..."

Isla leaned in, waiting for him to finish.

"A witch," Kael said at last, his voice barely above a whisper.

Isla's eyes widened, and for a moment, she was speechless. "A witch?" she repeated, incredulous. "Are you serious?"

Kael nodded again, his heart pounding in his chest. He expected her to react with fear, or worse, to tell their father. But instead, Isla's face softened, and she crossed her arms, considering his words.

"Well," she said after a long pause, "that's certainly unexpected."

Kael blinked, taken aback by her calm response. "You're... not going to tell Father?"

Isla shook her head. "Of course not. Do you think I want to see you locked in a tower for consorting with witches?" She frowned, her tone turning serious. "But Kael, you know how dangerous this is. Father's hatred for witches is deep. If he finds out—"

"I know," Kael interrupted, his frustration rising. "But she's not like what we've been told. She's... different. I don't know how to explain it, but I don't believe she's a threat."

Isla studied him closely, her expression thoughtful. "You care for her, don't you?"

Kael didn't answer immediately. He hadn't allowed himself to fully admit it, but now, standing here with his sister, the truth was undeniable. "I think I do."

Isla sighed, her face softening with concern. "Kael, this isn't a game. If Father even suspects you've been involved with a witch..."

"I know," Kael said again, his voice firm. "But I can't just forget about her."

Isla was quiet for a moment, then she placed a hand on his arm. "Just be careful, Kael. You're playing with fire, and I don't want to see you burned."

Kael nodded, grateful for her understanding. But even as his sister's words echoed in his mind, he knew he couldn't turn back. Something had been set in motion the night he met Elara, and he was powerless to stop it now.

The Heir of Two Worlds

Chapter 3:
The Kingdom's Fear

The sound of heavy boots echoed through the grand halls of the castle as King Ardan stormed into the war chamber. The room was already filled with high-ranking lords and military commanders, each of them watching in tense silence as the king took his place at the head of the long table. His face, usually a mask of calm authority, was contorted with frustration.

"My scouts have returned with disturbing news," King Ardan began, his voice low but filled with menace. "There have been sightings of magic near our borders. Witches are lurking closer than we thought."

The murmurs of the gathered men rose like a wave, crashing against the stone walls of the chamber. Kael, standing at the back of the room, listened carefully but kept his face impassive. His father's words, though grim, held a seed of untruth. He knew the supposed threat his father spoke of had little to do with the kind of magic he had encountered. He had seen Elara's power, and while it was formidable, it was not the menace the kingdom feared.

"These witches will stop at nothing to undermine the peace we have worked so hard to build," King Ardan continued, slamming his fist on the table. "They seek to corrupt our lands and our people with their vile sorcery. We cannot allow this."

The Heir of Two Worlds

One of the lords, an older man named Lord Harwin, leaned forward, his eyes dark with concern. "What would you have us do, Your Majesty? We've kept watch over the border for years, but they grow bolder. Should we strike now?"

The king's gaze swept over the room, his eyes sharp as a blade. "We will not wait for them to attack. We will strike first, and we will rid our kingdom of their taint once and for all."

Kael felt a knot form in his stomach. His father was preparing for war—a war built on fear and misunderstanding. He wanted to speak out, to tell his father that not all magic was evil, but he knew it would be futile. The king's mind was already made up.

"Father," Kael said, stepping forward, his voice measured, "we have no proof that the witches intend to attack. Perhaps we should seek a peaceful resolution before resorting to violence."

All eyes turned to him, the room going deadly silent. Kael could feel the tension in the air, and he knew his words had caused a ripple. His father's gaze darkened, and for a moment, Kael thought he might lash out in anger.

"A peaceful resolution?" King Ardan repeated, his voice icy. "You think these witches can be reasoned with, Kael? Have you forgotten the damage they've done in the past? The lives lost because of their treachery?"

Kael clenched his fists, keeping his voice steady. "I only mean that we may not fully understand their intentions. Not all witches seek harm. We must—"

"Enough!" Ardan's voice thundered, cutting him off. "I will not tolerate sympathy for those who practice dark magic, especially not in this chamber."

Kael fell silent, his jaw tight with frustration. His father was impossible to reason with on matters of magic, especially when the kingdom's safety was concerned. Ardan's hatred for witches ran deeper than just fear—it was personal, though Kael didn't know the full story. He had heard whispers in his youth about how the king had lost someone close to him due to witchcraft, but the details were shrouded in mystery.

"I will not allow this kingdom to fall prey to their wickedness," Ardan said, his tone final. "We prepare for war."

Kael's heart sank as he watched the lords around the table nodding in agreement. The momentum of fear was too strong to stop now. His father had made up his mind, and the council would not dare to oppose him.

But Kael couldn't sit by and watch this happen. He had to find a way to stop the war before it began. And to do that, he needed to find Elara again.

That night, Kael slipped out of the castle under the cover of darkness. He knew the patrol schedules well enough to avoid detection as he made his way to the stables. His horse, a sleek black stallion named Storm, waited for him with quiet patience. As he mounted, he couldn't shake the feeling that he was being watched.

The journey to the forest was swift, the familiar path winding through the dense trees. Kael's heart raced with anticipation and anxiety. He hadn't been able to stop thinking about Elara since their last meeting, and now, more than ever, he needed to see her.

When he reached the clearing where they had met before, the forest was eerily silent. The moon bathed the area in pale light, casting long shadows over the ground. Kael dismounted, his eyes scanning the darkness for any sign of her.

"Elara," he called softly, his voice barely louder than a whisper. "I need to speak with you."

For a moment, there was no response, only the rustle of leaves in the wind. But then, as if she had been waiting for him all along, Elara stepped out from behind the trees, her violet eyes glowing faintly in the moonlight. She moved with the grace of someone who was part of the very forest itself, her green cloak blending seamlessly with the night.

"You've returned," she said, her voice soft but steady.

Kael nodded, stepping toward her. "I didn't have a choice. My father—he's preparing for war. He believes the witches are planning an attack."

Elara's expression remained calm, though Kael could see the flicker of sadness in her eyes. "And what do you believe, Prince?"

Kael swallowed hard, searching for the right words. "I don't know what to believe. But I know you're not the threat he thinks you are."

Elara's lips curved into a small, bitter smile. "Your father is not alone in his fear. Most of your people would rather see us destroyed than try to understand us."

"I don't want that," Kael said, his voice firm. "I came to you because I want to find a way to stop this. There has to be another way."

Elara studied him in silence, her eyes searching his for something unspoken. After what felt like an eternity, she spoke. "There is another way, but it is dangerous."

Kael's heart raced. "Tell me."

Elara stepped closer, her voice dropping to a whisper. "There is a power older than both our worlds, a magic that binds all things. If we can tap into it, we may be able to stop this war before it begins. But it comes at a cost."

"What kind of cost?" Kael asked, his brow furrowing.

Elara hesitated, her violet eyes darkening. "Magic like this demands balance. For every action, there is a consequence. If we succeed, it may change everything—your kingdom, your father, even you."

Kael took a deep breath, feeling the weight of her words settle on his shoulders. "I don't care about the risks. I'll do whatever it takes to stop this war."

Elara nodded slowly, though her eyes held a sadness Kael didn't fully understand. "Then we must act quickly. The forces at play are already in motion. If we fail..."

She didn't finish the sentence, but Kael understood. If they failed, it wouldn't just be a war—they could lose everything.

"Tell me what I need to do," he said, his voice steady despite the fear gnawing at him.

Elara reached out, her hand brushing lightly against his. "We'll need to gather the magic from the ancient places—places where the boundary between this world and the magical one is thin. But we'll need more than just power. We'll need trust."

Kael met her gaze, his heart pounding. "You have my trust."

Elara's expression softened for the briefest of moments. "Then let's begin."

Chapter 4:
The Witch's Dilemma

Elara stood at the edge of the clearing, her back to Kael as she stared into the dense forest. The trees whispered in the wind, carrying with them the voices of the ancient magic that permeated this place. She had always felt at home here, but tonight, the weight of the task ahead filled her with unease.

The moonlight bathed the clearing in a silvery glow, and though Kael was beside her, the distance between their worlds had never felt so vast. She could sense his determination, the resolve in his voice when he said he was ready to risk everything to stop the war. But she knew what he didn't—the true cost of the magic they were about to invoke.

"I need to tell you something, Kael," Elara said quietly, her voice barely above a whisper.

Kael stepped closer, his presence a steady warmth in the cool night air. "What is it?"

Elara took a deep breath, turning to face him. "There's a reason the witches have stayed hidden for so long. The magic we are about to summon is powerful, but it's also unpredictable. It doesn't obey the rules of the world as you know them. If we misuse it, the consequences could be... devastating."

Kael's brow furrowed, his gaze steady. "You're worried."

"Of course I'm worried," Elara replied, her violet eyes locking onto his. "I've seen what this magic can do. It can tear apart everything we've built—everything we love."

Kael's face softened as he reached for her hand, his touch gentle but firm. "I trust you, Elara. I believe you can control it. We can control it, together."

Elara's heart ached at his words. She wanted to believe him. She wanted to believe that, together, they could shape the future—one where witches and humans lived in peace, where their love could exist without fear. But the truth was far more complicated. Magic had its own will, and it didn't care for love or peace.

Her hesitation must have shown on her face because Kael squeezed her hand, his eyes searching hers. "You don't have to do this alone."

Elara looked away, the memories of her coven flashing through her mind. The witches who had raised her had warned her about falling for someone like Kael—someone who belonged to the very world that had persecuted them for centuries. They had been clear: to protect the witches, she must stay far from the humans who feared their power.

But it was already too late for that.

"I wish it were that simple," Elara said, pulling her hand away. "My coven won't accept this. They won't accept you. If they find out what we're doing..."

Kael's expression hardened. "Then we'll make them understand. If they want peace, we're offering them a way to end the fighting. They must see that."

Elara shook her head, frustration bubbling to the surface. "It's not that easy, Kael! They don't trust humans. And why should they? Look at what your father has done to us—hunted us, driven us to the edges of the world, treating us like we're monsters."

Kael was silent for a moment, his jaw clenched. "I'm not my father."

"I know," Elara said softly, her anger fading as quickly as it had come. "But the world doesn't see that. To them, you're the crown prince of a kingdom that wants to destroy everything we are."

Kael's gaze darkened as he stepped closer. "Then let's prove them wrong."

Elara studied him for a long moment, her heart torn between the life she had always known and the one she dared to imagine with him. She had lived her entire life on the run, hiding from a world that feared her magic. But now, with Kael at her side, a glimmer of hope sparked inside her.

Could they truly change the world together? Could their love be enough to bridge the chasm between their people?

But even as she clung to that hope, the reality of her situation loomed large. Her coven was more than just her family—it was her home, her duty. If she chose Kael, she would be turning her back on everything she had been raised to protect. And worse, she would be putting the witches in danger.

"I need time," she said finally, her voice barely above a whisper.

Kael's expression softened, and he nodded. "I understand."

Elara turned away, her heart heavy with the weight of her decision. She couldn't keep Kael waiting for long. The forces moving against them wouldn't allow it. But before she could choose her path, she needed to return to the coven. She needed to face the witches who had taught her everything and ask for their guidance—even if she already knew what their answer would be.

The journey back to the coven's hidden sanctuary was swift, though every step filled Elara with a growing sense of dread. The witches lived deep within the heart of the forest, their home shielded by powerful enchantments that kept outsiders away. Only those who carried the bloodline of witches could pass through the barriers unharmed.

As Elara approached the entrance, she felt the familiar hum of magic in the air. The trees seemed to shift around her, their branches bending to create a path that led her into the heart of the coven. The sanctuary was a vast grove, hidden beneath the canopy of towering trees, where the air always felt cool and charged with energy.

The other witches were already gathered, their faces illuminated by the soft glow of enchanted lanterns hanging from the trees. At the center of the group stood Maelis, the eldest of the witches and the leader of the coven. Her long silver hair flowed down her back, and her eyes, though clouded with age, gleamed with sharp intelligence.

"Elara," Maelis said, her voice strong despite her years. "You've returned sooner than expected."

Elara hesitated, stepping forward. "I need your guidance, Maelis."

The other witches watched her in silence, their expressions unreadable. They could sense that something had changed, though they didn't yet know the full extent of it.

Maelis gestured for her to continue. "What troubles you, child?"

Elara took a deep breath, her hands trembling slightly as she spoke. "I've found a way to stop the war. But it's dangerous. It requires magic from the ancient places, and... it involves someone from the kingdom."

A murmur spread through the witches, their eyes widening in disbelief. Maelis' gaze sharpened. "Someone from the kingdom? Who?"

Elara hesitated, then spoke the truth. "Prince Kael."

A stunned silence fell over the grove, and the tension in the air thickened. Maelis' expression darkened, and the other witches exchanged nervous glances.

"You've been consorting with the prince?" one of the younger witches, Ayla, asked, her voice filled with accusation. "Do you know what you've done?"

Elara stood her ground, though her heart raced. "I haven't betrayed you. I'm trying to find a way to save us."

"By trusting the son of the man who seeks to destroy us?" Maelis' voice was cold, her gaze hard as she studied Elara. "Do you truly believe the prince can be trusted?"

Elara's chest tightened, but she met Maelis' gaze without wavering. "I do. He's not like his father. He wants to stop the war as much as we do. If we work together, we can—"

"No!" Maelis snapped, her voice ringing out through the grove. "You are blinded by your feelings, Elara. You forget your duty to the coven, to your sisters. This prince is a danger to us all, whether you believe it or not."

Elara's heart sank, but she refused to back down. "I won't let this war destroy everything. We have a chance to stop it, but only if we're willing to take the risk."

Maelis studied her for a long, tense moment, and then her expression softened with something that looked like sorrow. "You have always been strong-willed, Elara. But this path you've chosen will only lead to ruin. You must sever your ties with the prince before it is too late."

Elara's throat tightened, the weight of her leader's words crushing her. She had known this would be the answer, but hearing it spoken aloud made the reality of it unbearable. If she chose Kael, she would lose the only family she had ever known. But if she turned her back on him, the war would continue, and countless lives would be lost.

She was trapped between two worlds, and no matter which path she chose, something would be lost.

"I need more time," Elara whispered, though she wasn't sure to whom she was speaking—Maelis, the coven, or herself.

But time was running out.

Chapter 5:
A Royal Engagement

As the sun rose over the kingdom, bathing the landscape in a warm, golden hue, Kael stood quietly in the gardens, lost in contemplation. The weight of his father's words still echoed in his mind: duty, loyalty, alliance. These were the tenets he had been raised to honor, yet they now felt like shackles, binding him to a fate he couldn't accept.

Elara's vision lingered in his thoughts—the hope of peace, the promise of something more than war and obligation. But the reality of his duties loomed large, the expectations of an entire kingdom pressing down on him. The impending engagement to Princess Rhea weighed heavily on his heart, intensifying the turmoil within.

His sister, Isla, had listened patiently as he confided in her about Elara, her understanding providing a small measure of comfort. She had offered a grim truth—that he could not delay his decision much longer, lest it be made for him. But even with her support, the choice seemed no clearer.

The rustle of leaves in the garden drew Kael's attention, and he turned to see Rhea approaching with graceful poise. Her gown shimmered with the colors of the rising sun, every bit the royal princess expected of her. Her eyes held a quiet strength, though they betrayed a flicker of uncertainty as she regarded him.

"Kael," Rhea greeted him, her voice calm and even, "I hoped I might find you here."

He offered a nod, though words seemed to evade him. The complexities of their situation hung unspoken between them, understood yet unaddressed.

"I imagine this is difficult for you," Rhea continued, her gaze unwavering. "It is for me as well. I know our engagement was arranged for political gain and not out of love."

Kael glanced down, the truth of her words resonating within him. "I don't wish to deceive you," he said, choosing honesty. "My heart belongs elsewhere."

Rhea's expression softened, though there was no anger in her eyes. "And yet, here we are, bound by duty to uphold this alliance. Our families see it as necessary, especially with the tensions we face."

He met her gaze, a silent understanding passing between them. She, too, was a player in this political game, and neither of them had been given a choice.

"I don't wish to force you into a marriage that brings you no joy," Rhea said softly, surprising him with her sincerity. "But neither of us can deny the responsibilities we've been born into."

Kael took a deep breath, the reality of his predicament settling like a stone in his chest. "I must find a way to honor my duty without forsaking what I truly believe in."

Rhea considered him for a moment, then nodded. "Perhaps we can speak with your father together. Present a united front, showing him that this engagement may not be the best path."

Encouraged by her willingness to support him, Kael felt a flicker of hope. "Thank you, Rhea. Your understanding means more than I can say."

She smiled faintly, though her expression remained thoughtful. "We are both bound by the expectations of others, but together, maybe we can find another path."

With a renewed sense of purpose, Kael resolved to seek his father's counsel, knowing that he needed more than words to sway the king's mind. The specter of war loomed on the horizon, and with it, the fate of the witches and the kingdom. But if there was a chance to change the tide, he would seize it.

As Kael returned to the castle, his decision made, he felt a twinge of uncertainty but also a newfound resolve. His journey was far from over, and the trials ahead would demand courage and conviction unlike any he had ever faced. Yet with allies like Isla and Rhea, and his faith in Elara, he dared to hope for a future beyond the shadows that threatened his world.

Arianna Reed

Chapter 6:
Shadows and Pursuit

The moonlit winds wrapped around Kael and Elara as they soared across the night sky, leaving the chaos of the ballroom far behind. The world below them was a tapestry of forests and meadows, painted in shades of silver and blue. Yet, despite the breathtaking view, Kael's mind was a whirlwind of fear and uncertainty. They had acted on instinct, with no clear plan beyond their immediate escape.

Elara's grip on his hand was firm, and he could feel the power emanating from her, holding them aloft with her magic. Her expression was a mask of concentration, her violet eyes fixed on the horizon.

After what felt like an eternity, Elara released the magic, and they touched down in a secluded glade, hidden by towering trees that swayed gently in the wind. Kael staggered slightly upon landing, his legs unsteady from the flight. The cool night air was filled with the scent of earth and pine, a stark contrast to the heated tension of the ballroom.

"Are you okay?" Elara asked, concern threading her voice.

Kael nodded, the adrenaline still coursing through his veins. "Yeah, just... overwhelmed, I suppose."

Elara gave a small nod, understanding evident in her gaze. "We don't have much time. Your father will send troops after us. We need to keep moving."

Her words pulled him back to the present danger, and Kael's resolve hardened. He couldn't afford to let fear consume him. Not now. He looked at Elara, gratitude and determination mingling in his expression. "Thank you for coming for me."

A faint smile touched her lips, though it was tinged with sadness. "I couldn't leave you there. Not after everything."

For a moment, they stood in silence, the weight of their escape pressing upon them. Then, Elara gestured toward the thick shadows at the edge of the glade. "This way. There's a place we can hide, at least for the night."

They moved quickly and quietly through the forest, the night enveloping them like a cloak. The sound of crickets filled the air, and the leaves rustled softly underfoot. Despite the urgency of their flight, Kael felt a strange sense of calm. Elara's presence was a steadying force, guiding him through the darkness.

After what seemed like hours of walking, they arrived at a small, hidden cave nestled between ancient trees. The entrance was shrouded in vines, almost invisible to the untrained eye. Elara waved her hand, and the vines parted as if obeying her silent command.

Inside, the cave was surprisingly warm and dry. Elara whispered a few words, and a gentle, magical light filled the space, casting soft shadows on the walls.

"We can rest here until dawn," she said, her voice echoing softly. "It's safe. I've used this place before."

Kael sank down onto the cool stone floor, exhaustion finally catching up with him. He leaned back against the wall, closing his eyes for a moment. "What are we going to do, Elara?" he murmured, uncertainty creeping into his voice.

Elara sat beside him, her gaze fixed on the small orb of light floating above them. "We need to gather allies. People who understand and believe in what we're trying to do. There are those within the kingdom who oppose your father's war. We must find them and rally support."

Kael opened his eyes, looking at her with renewed hope. "You think we can do it? Convince them to stand with us?"

Elara's expression was thoughtful, yet determined. "I believe we have to try. There's more at stake here than just us. It's about changing the tide, proving that magic and humans can coexist without fear."

Kael nodded, feeling a warmth spread through his chest. It was a daunting task, fraught with peril, but he knew they couldn't turn back now. Their journey was just beginning, and the path ahead, though uncertain, was one they would travel together.

As the night wore on, they talked quietly, forming plans and sharing their hopes and fears. Outside the cave, the forest stood in serene silence, a world untouched by the turmoil that threatened their lives. And as the first hints of dawn touched the sky, Kael felt a spark of optimism—fragile but real. They had each other, and that was enough, for now.

As they settled into the silence, both exhausted and alert to the dangers lurking beyond the sanctuary of the cave, Kael allowed himself a brief moment of rest. But sleep would not come easily, for the events of the night still danced vividly in his mind.

Elara, sensing his restlessness, reached for his hand, a silent promise in her touch. The gesture was small, yet it conveyed strength and companionship—everything they would need in the days to come.

And as the sun slowly rose, painting the sky with bands of gold and pink, Kael held on to that promise, determined to see their journey through to the end.

Chapter 7:
The Safe Haven

The night air rushed past them as Elara's magic carried Kael and herself far from the castle, the wind howling like a wild beast at their heels. Kael's heart raced, his mind still reeling from the chaos they had left behind. His father's fury, the accusations of treason, and the looks of shock on the faces of the guests all swirled together in his thoughts. But now, all that mattered was Elara and the freedom they had fought for.

They soared over the vast forests that bordered the kingdom, the trees below stretching endlessly into the distance. Kael had no idea where they were going, but he trusted Elara's magic to guide them. Her grip on his hand was strong, a silent reassurance that they were in this together.

After what felt like hours, Elara gently lowered them to the ground, the wind dying down as they landed in a secluded clearing deep within the forest. The trees here were ancient, their twisted branches reaching toward the sky like silent sentinels. A small stream trickled nearby, its soothing sound the only noise in the stillness of the night.

Kael released a shaky breath, his legs weak from the flight. He turned to Elara, who was already scanning their surroundings with cautious eyes. "Where are we?" he asked, his voice low.

Elara gestured toward the trees. "This is a sanctuary—a place hidden from both the kingdom and the coven. Few know of its existence. We should be safe here, for now."

Kael looked around, the quiet beauty of the clearing slowly calming his racing heart. "Safe," he echoed, though the word felt foreign to him now. After everything that had happened, he wasn't sure if they would ever truly be safe again.

Elara stepped closer, her violet eyes filled with concern. "I'm sorry, Kael. I didn't mean for any of this to happen."

Kael shook his head, reaching for her hand. "You don't need to apologize. None of this is your fault. If anything, I should have been more careful. I underestimated how far my father would go."

Elara squeezed his hand, her touch grounding him. "We couldn't have predicted Gareth's betrayal. Someone must have seen us that night. But it doesn't matter now. We're here, and we'll find a way forward."

Kael nodded, though the weight of the situation still pressed heavily on his chest. "My father won't stop until he finds us. He'll send every knight in the kingdom after us."

"I know," Elara said softly. "But we have time. The magic of this place will keep us hidden for a while. It's protected by ancient spells that even your father's most powerful mages can't break."

Kael glanced around the clearing, feeling the subtle hum of magic in the air. It was different from the kind of magic he had witnessed in the kingdom—more primal, more connected to the earth itself. He could feel its power, like a heartbeat thrumming beneath the surface.

"How long do you think we have?" Kael asked, his voice heavy with the uncertainty of their future.

Elara's expression darkened. "Not long. A few days, maybe more, but we can't stay here forever. Eventually, we'll need to make a move."

Kael frowned, his thoughts racing. "Where will we go? The kingdom will hunt us, and I'm sure your coven won't be pleased with you for being with me."

Elara looked away, her face tense. "No, they won't. In their eyes, I've betrayed them by trusting a human, especially a prince. They'll see me as a threat now."

Kael's heart ached at her words. He hated that she had to choose between him and her people, just as he had to choose between her and his kingdom. "I won't let them hurt you," he said firmly. "We'll figure this out together."

Elara gave him a sad smile. "I know you mean that, but the forces against us are greater than either of us can fully understand. My coven's magic runs deep, and your father's reach extends far beyond the borders of the kingdom. We're caught in the middle of something much larger than ourselves."

Kael's frustration grew. He hated feeling powerless, hated knowing that they were being hunted from both sides. But as he looked into Elara's eyes, he knew one thing for certain—he wouldn't give her up. He couldn't.

"We'll find a way," Kael said, his voice filled with determination. "There has to be a way to stop this war before it destroys everything."

Elara hesitated, her gaze searching his face for something unspoken. Then she nodded. "There is one way, but it's dangerous."

Kael's heart skipped a beat. "What is it?"

Elara looked away, her face conflicted. "There's a place, deep within the mountains, where ancient magic sleeps. It's older than the coven, older than the kingdom itself. It's said that whoever awakens that magic will have the power to change the world."

Kael frowned. "Change the world? How?"

Elara's voice lowered, as if she were revealing a long-buried secret. "The magic is a force of balance. It can end the war, reshape the kingdom, and forge a new path for both humans and witches. But it's unpredictable. It doesn't bend to the will of those who seek it—it demands sacrifice."

Kael's breath caught in his throat. "What kind of sacrifice?"

Elara turned back to him, her eyes filled with a mixture of hope and fear. "I don't know. No one has ever tried to awaken it. But if we want to stop the war, it might be our only chance."

Kael stared at her, the weight of her words sinking in. This magic she spoke of—it was dangerous, but it could be the key to everything. It could be the answer they had been searching for. But at what cost?

"We have to try," Kael said, his voice firm despite the uncertainty in his heart. "We can't let this war tear our worlds apart."

Elara nodded, though the fear in her eyes lingered. "Then we need to leave soon. The journey to the mountains is treacherous, and we'll be vulnerable along the way. But if we're careful, we might be able to reach it before anyone realizes where we've gone."

Kael took a deep breath, steeling himself for what lay ahead. "Then let's get ready. We'll leave at first light."

Elara turned to him, her gaze softening. "Kael... thank you. For trusting me."

Kael smiled, though his heart was heavy with the weight of their future. "I trust you with everything."

For the rest of the night, they made preparations in the quiet of the sanctuary. Elara gathered the few magical supplies she could find, while Kael scouted the perimeter of the clearing, making sure they wouldn't be ambushed in the middle of the night. The air was thick with tension, but there was also a sense of purpose between them. They knew what they had to do.

As the first light of dawn crept over the horizon, Kael and Elara stood side by side at the edge of the clearing. The journey ahead was uncertain, but they were ready to face it together.

"Are you ready?" Elara asked, her voice quiet.

Kael looked out at the forest, the mountains looming in the distance like silent guardians. He knew the path ahead would be difficult, but he also knew he had no other choice.

"I'm ready," he said, his voice steady. "Let's go."

With that, they set off into the unknown, their hearts heavy with the weight of what was to come.

Chapter 8:
The Child of Prophecy

The journey to the mountains was long and grueling. Days passed in a blur of dense forests, rocky paths, and icy winds as Kael and Elara pressed on, driven by the weight of the mission they had chosen. The mountains loomed ever closer, their jagged peaks piercing the sky like ancient sentinels. But as they traveled deeper into the wilderness, something else began to stir—something neither of them had fully expected.

Elara had grown quiet over the past few days, her usual confidence tempered by a growing unease. Kael noticed it in the way she moved, slower and more deliberate than usual, and in the way she held her stomach when she thought he wasn't looking.

"Elara," Kael said gently as they paused to rest by a riverbank one evening, the setting sun casting a golden glow over the landscape, "you've been different these past few days. Is something wrong?"

Elara looked up, her violet eyes meeting his with a mixture of hesitation and fear. She had been holding this secret for longer than she wanted to admit, but now, standing here with him, she could no longer hide it.

"I didn't want to tell you like this," she said softly, her hand resting on her abdomen. "But you need to know. Kael... I'm pregnant."

Kael froze, his mind struggling to process the words. Pregnant? He stared at Elara, searching her face for any sign that this was some misunderstanding or mistake. But there was none. Her eyes held nothing but truth.

"You're... pregnant?" he repeated, his voice barely above a whisper.

Elara nodded, her expression uncertain. "I've known for a little while, but I wasn't sure how to tell you, especially with everything going on. I didn't want to distract you from the mission."

Kael's heart raced, his emotions swirling in a storm of shock, joy, and fear. A child. His child. With Elara. The realization hit him like a tidal wave, and for a moment, he couldn't speak.

Finally, he stepped closer, his hand gently covering hers on her stomach. "Elara... why didn't you tell me sooner?"

"I didn't want to add to your burden," she said softly, her voice tinged with regret. "But I should have. I'm sorry."

Kael shook his head, his heart swelling with emotion. "No, you don't need to apologize. I just... I wish I'd known. This changes everything."

Elara's eyes darkened with worry. "I know. That's why I was afraid to tell you. The child complicates things—our journey, the danger we're facing. And there's more, Kael."

Kael frowned, his chest tightening at the uncertainty in her voice. "What do you mean?"

Elara hesitated, her gaze shifting to the distant mountains. "This child... it's not just any child. There are prophecies about a union between a witch and a human of royal blood. The child of such a union is said to possess immense power, a power that could either unite the two worlds or tear them apart."

Kael's blood ran cold. "A prophecy? About our child?"

Elara nodded, her voice filled with quiet sorrow. "Yes. I didn't realize it at first, but I've been dreaming about it. Visions of our child standing at a crossroads, choosing between light and darkness. I don't know what it means, but the magic surrounding this pregnancy is... different."

Kael took a deep breath, trying to steady himself. He had faced wars, battles, and his father's wrath, but nothing had prepared him for this. The thought of their child—his child—being at the center of a prophecy that could determine the fate of the world was terrifying.

"What do we do?" he asked, his voice raw with emotion. "How do we protect our child from this?"

Elara looked down, her hand resting on her stomach protectively. "I don't know. But I do know that we can't go back. The coven will want the child for its power, and your father... he'll see the child as a threat. We can't trust anyone."

Kael felt a wave of helplessness crash over him. His family, the kingdom, even Elara's own people—no one could be trusted with the knowledge of their child. They were alone in this.

"We'll figure it out," Kael said, though the weight of his words felt immense. "We'll protect our child. No matter what."

Elara gave him a sad smile, though her eyes held the same determination he had always admired in her. "We will. But we also need to reach the ancient magic. It may be our only hope of finding a way to keep our child safe and stop this war."

Kael nodded, though the path ahead felt even more daunting than before. The stakes had risen higher than he had ever imagined. Not only were they fighting for peace between two worlds, but now they were fighting for the future of their child—an innocent life that could tip the balance of power in ways neither of them fully understood.

The following days passed in a haze of anxious anticipation. Every step closer to the mountains felt heavier, every glance shared between Kael and Elara filled with unspoken fears. They knew the danger they were walking into, but they had no choice. The prophecy hung over them like a shadow, its weight growing with each passing moment.

At night, Elara's dreams grew more vivid, filled with images of their child—an enigmatic figure standing between two paths, one leading to light and the other to darkness. In the dreams, the child's face was always obscured, their features blurred by magic, but the power emanating from them was undeniable. It was a power that could reshape the world, for better or worse.

Kael began to dream too, though his dreams were darker. He saw his father's army marching through the kingdom, flames rising in the distance as war consumed everything he had once known. In the distance, he could hear the cries of their child, but no matter how hard he tried, he could never reach them in time.

When they finally reached the base of the mountains, the air grew colder, and the path ahead steeper. The ancient magic that Elara had spoken of seemed to hum beneath the surface, a primal force waiting to be awakened. But as they climbed higher, a new fear gnawed at Kael—what if they weren't the only ones seeking this power?

"Elara," Kael said as they stopped to rest on a rocky ledge overlooking the vast expanse below. "Do you think anyone else knows about this magic? Could the coven or my father's mages be after it too?"

Elara's eyes darkened, her gaze fixed on the mountain's peak. "It's possible. Magic this old calls to those who seek power. But we're ahead of them for now. We have to reach it before they do."

Kael nodded, though the feeling of being hunted still lingered. They weren't just fighting time—they were fighting against forces that neither of them fully understood. But as he looked at Elara, her strength and determination unwavering despite the burden of the prophecy, he knew they couldn't turn back.

They had come too far.

"Whatever happens," Kael said, taking her hand, "we'll face it together. For us. And for our child."

Elara smiled, though the fear in her eyes remained. "Together."

As they continued their ascent, the wind howled around them, carrying with it the whispers of ancient magic. Kael knew that they were nearing the source, the place where everything would change. But as the prophecy loomed larger in his mind, one question remained unanswered—what choice would their child make when the time came? Would they follow the path of light, or would the darkness consume them?

For now, all Kael and Elara could do was keep moving forward, one step at a time, toward an uncertain future.

Chapter 9:
Whispers of War

The air was thin and biting as Kael and Elara climbed higher into the desolate peaks of the mountains. The sky above them was a canvas of swirling gray, obscuring the sun and casting a pallor over the rocky terrain. They pressed on, their breaths coming in ragged gasps, each step a battle against the chill that seeped into their bones.

Despite the fatigue pulling at them, an unspoken resolve knit them together. The ancient magic that pulsed beneath the ground was a constant hum in their senses, guiding them toward the source they desperately sought. They had little else to rely on, the world behind them filled with chaos and the specter of a looming war.

In the capital, however, King Ardan was far from idle. Pacing the war chamber, the king's hardened eyes flickered as the councilmen echoed the rumors of his son's vanishing. Ardan's emotions warred within him—betrayal and anger mingling with a glimmer of paternal concern.

"They've vanished into thin air," Gareth reported, his voice steady despite the fury he sensed in the room. "Our search parties have come up empty-handed."

A scowl darkened Ardan's features. "You will find him," he ordered, his tone a low growl. "Kael's actions have left me no choice. The witch's sorcery can only shield them for so long."

Lord Rowen cleared his throat, approaching with caution. "Sire, whispers speak of the prince and the witch heading toward the mountains. There's talk of ancient magic there, a power that could change everything."

Ardan ground his teeth, his eyes narrowing. "Power indeed," he mused, more to himself than those surrounding him. "Make no mistake, Kael is ensnared by her sorcery. He shan't wield that power against us."

The room fell into an uneasy silence, Ardan's commands hanging heavily in the air. "Dispatch more troops, Gareth. Search every crevice of this kingdom. Prepare the army, should Kael dare to wield that power, we will be ready."

Gareth saluted crisply, a grim determination etched on his face. "Yes, Your Majesty."

Back in the mountains, the sharp rocks underfoot proved treacherous. Elara stumbled slightly, clutching her belly protectively, while Kael moved to steady her, worry etched on his brow.

"We're close," Elara breathed, her voice a whisper between panting breaths. "The magic is stronger here."

Kael nodded, though uncertainty twisted in his gut. "What do we do when we find it? Can we even control it?"

Elara hesitated, biting her lip. "I do not know. This magic... it is wild. It may help us or turn against us."

The path narrowed further, the landscape echoing with a deep, ominous sound as if the mountains themselves held their collective breath. Above them, the sky churned, the air electric with potential.

"We'll find a way," Kael resolved, determination setting in his jaw. "We have to, for everyone's sake."

Elara nodded silently, though the anxiety in her eyes remained. "We may already be too late."

As if in answer, the mountain rumbled, a deep resonance that tugged them forward. Elara grasped Kael's hand, and they climbed faster, the urgency of their mission spurring every step.

They reached the plateau, breathless and wary, where a stark monument of stone awaited them—a monolith etched with ancient runes shimmering with magic untapped for centuries.

"Here we are," Elara breathed, awe mingling with fear in her voice. "The heart of the ancient magic."

But their anticipation froze into shock as a figure stepped out from the shadows, unfolding with the inescapable presence of authority.

"Elara," Maelis shot the name through the silence, his tone a mixture of reproach and disappointment. "You stand on the brink of betrayal. A human here, on this sacred ground?"

Elara squared her shoulders, defiance in her stance. "I came to stop this madness. The magic must be used wisely, Maelis—it's our only hope for peace."

Maelis's eyes turned stormy, his gaze a burning scrutiny. "You've become blinded by idealism, not wisdom. This child born of human and witch blood bears a prophecy to destroy us."

Kael's heart clenched, his fears coalescing into reality. "Maelis, this magic—it can be hope, not destruction. Unite our worlds, not divide them."

"You tempt fate," Maelis warned, his form growing fierce with power. "You think to harness what you don't understand?"

The tension reached a breaking point as the ground quaked, the light of the runes flickering like a flame in the wind. Maelis's silhouette shifted, a vortex gathering at his fingertips.

"I won't let this prophecy unfold," Maelis spoke, a warning layered with fear. He cast out his hands, unleashing a storm of dark magic with a crash akin to thunder.

Chapter 10:
The Dark Forest

Maelis' dark magic hurtled toward Kael and Elara with terrifying speed, crackling through the air like a bolt of lightning. Instinctively, Kael threw himself in front of Elara, raising his arms as if he could shield her from the blast. But before the magic could strike, Elara reacted, her own hands rising in a blur of motion. A shimmering barrier of light appeared between them, absorbing the impact of Maelis' attack with a deafening crash.

The force of the collision sent shockwaves through the plateau, and Kael staggered backward, barely keeping his footing as the ground trembled beneath them. Elara's face was pale, her concentration fierce as she struggled to maintain the barrier.

"Run!" she shouted to Kael, her voice strained. "I'll hold him off!"

But Kael wasn't about to leave her. He grabbed her arm, his heart racing. "I'm not leaving you! We do this together!"

Maelis sneered, his silver hair flowing wildly in the wind as he summoned another wave of magic. "You think you can stop me? You've always been a fool, Elara, but now you're delusional. This is beyond you."

Elara gritted her teeth, sweat beading on her brow as the strain of holding off Maelis' power took its toll. "Maybe," she said through clenched teeth, "but I won't let you harm our child."

At her words, Maelis' eyes narrowed, a dangerous gleam in his gaze. "You've sealed your fate, Elara. You and that child are a threat to everything we've built. I'll stop you, even if it means destroying you both."

Kael's heart lurched at the threat, and he stepped forward, drawing his sword. He had no magic of his own, but he wasn't helpless. "If you want to hurt her, you'll have to go through me."

Maelis barely spared him a glance. "You, Prince? You think you can stand against me with a sword?"

Without warning, Maelis flicked his wrist, and Kael felt a sharp pull at his chest as dark tendrils of magic wrapped around him, lifting him off the ground. He gasped, struggling against the invisible force as it tightened around him like a noose, squeezing the air from his lungs.

"Kael!" Elara screamed, her voice filled with panic as she reached for him.

Maelis' expression twisted into a cruel smile. "It ends here, Elara. This is what happens when you betray your own kind."

But just as the dark magic began to crush the life from Kael, a brilliant burst of light erupted from Elara's hands. The tendrils of Maelis' magic disintegrated, and Kael fell to the ground, gasping for breath. Elara's power surged, her violet eyes glowing with intensity as she stepped between Kael and Maelis.

"You're wrong, Maelis," Elara said, her voice low but steady. "It's not betrayal to seek peace. It's not betrayal to love."

With that, Elara unleashed a wave of pure, blinding light. The force of her magic hit Maelis like a tidal wave, sending him staggering backward. He tried to resist, but Elara's power was too strong. He fell to his knees, his face twisted with fury and disbelief as the light overwhelmed him.

"You'll regret this," Maelis snarled as the light engulfed him. "The prophecy will destroy you all."

With a final roar, he vanished, consumed by the magic that had once been his greatest weapon.

The plateau fell silent, the air heavy with the aftermath of the battle. Kael struggled to his feet, his chest heaving as he rushed to Elara's side. "Are you okay?" he asked, his voice hoarse.

Elara nodded, though she looked exhausted. "I'm fine," she said, her voice barely above a whisper. "But we need to keep moving. Maelis may be gone, but others will come. We don't have much time."

Kael's heart still pounded from the battle, but he knew she was right. The ancient magic had been awakened, and it wouldn't be long before others sensed it. They had to reach it before anyone else.

He wrapped his arm around Elara's waist, helping her as they made their way toward the monolith. The runes on the stone glowed brighter now, pulsating with power. The air around them crackled with energy, and Kael could feel the magic thrumming beneath his skin.

"This is it," Elara whispered, her eyes wide as they stood before the monolith. "The ancient magic."

Kael stared at the stone, his heart racing. They had come so far, risked everything to reach this moment. But now, standing before the source of unimaginable power, he felt a surge of doubt. What if they couldn't control it? What if it consumed them?

Elara reached out, her hand hovering over the runes. "Once I touch it," she said quietly, "there's no going back."

Kael placed his hand over hers, his voice steady. "We face it together. Whatever happens."

Elara nodded, her eyes filled with both fear and determination. Then, with a deep breath, she pressed her hand against the monolith.

The moment her skin touched the stone, a shockwave of magic exploded from the monolith, sending ripples of light across the plateau. The ground shook, and the air around them shimmered with power. Kael felt the magic surge through him, filling him with a strange, otherworldly energy.

Elara gasped, her body trembling as the magic coursed through her. "I can feel it," she whispered, her voice filled with awe. "It's... so powerful."

Kael held her steady, his own body buzzing with the force of the magic. But as the energy flowed through them, he noticed something else—something dark, lurking beneath the surface of the magic.

"Elara," Kael said, his voice filled with concern. "There's something wrong. The magic... it's not just power. There's something else."

Elara's eyes widened, and she pulled her hand away from the stone, her breath coming in quick, shallow gasps. "You're right," she whispered. "The magic is corrupted. It's been tainted by darkness."

Kael's heart sank. They had come here seeking a way to stop the war, to protect their child. But now, it seemed that the ancient magic itself was a danger—one they hadn't anticipated.

"What do we do?" Kael asked, his voice filled with dread.

Elara shook her head, her face pale. "I don't know. If we can't purify the magic, it could destroy everything."

Before they could say more, the wind picked up again, howling through the mountains. The air grew colder, and Kael felt a chill run down his spine.

"We're not alone," Elara said, her voice barely audible over the wind.

Kael turned, his hand gripping the hilt of his sword as he scanned the shadows. Figures began to emerge from the darkness—dozens of them. Some were cloaked in the familiar robes of the coven, their faces hidden beneath their hoods. Others wore the armor of the kingdom's soldiers, their swords gleaming in the moonlight.

At the head of the group stood a figure Kael recognized all too well.

His father.

King Ardan's face was a mask of cold fury as he approached, flanked by his knights. His eyes were locked on Kael, and the hatred in his gaze was unmistakable.

"Kael," the king said, his voice dripping with venom. "You've led us on quite a chase. But it ends here."

Kael's heart pounded in his chest as he stepped forward, positioning himself between Elara and his father. "It doesn't have to be like this," he said, his voice steady despite the fear gnawing at him. "We can end this war—together."

Ardan's lips curled into a sneer. "You've been poisoned by that witch's lies. You think you can control the ancient magic? You're a fool, Kael. You don't understand the forces you've unleashed."

Kael clenched his fists, his voice rising. "I understand more than you think. This isn't about power. It's about peace."

"Peace?" Ardan spat. "There will be no peace as long as witches like her exist."

Kael's heart sank, but he didn't back down. "If you destroy her, you destroy everything we could have. Our child—"

"Your child is an abomination!" Ardan shouted, his face contorted with rage. "It will bring ruin to this world!"

Kael's chest tightened with fury. "You're wrong, Father. The child is the key to peace."

Ardan's eyes blazed with hatred. "Then you leave me no choice."

The Heir of Two Worlds

He raised his hand, and the knights drew their swords, advancing toward Kael and Elara.

Kael drew his own blade, his heart pounding in his chest as he prepared for the fight of his life.

Chapter 11:
Lyra's Awakening

The moment King Ardan raised his hand and his knights began to advance, Kael's heart pounded in his chest. The gleam of swords and the grim determination on their faces left no doubt—his father had come to finish this. Kael glanced back at Elara, who stood behind him, her face pale but resolute. She knew, just as he did, that there was no turning back now.

"Stay behind me," Kael whispered, gripping the hilt of his sword.

Elara's violet eyes met his, and though she nodded, there was a fire in her gaze. "I won't let you fight alone."

Before Kael could respond, the knights charged, their armor clanking as they descended upon them. Kael raised his sword, blocking the first strike aimed at him, his muscles straining under the force. He deflected blow after blow, his movements driven by pure instinct and desperation. Every clang of steel against steel echoed like thunder across the mountaintop.

In the midst of the battle, Kael caught sight of his father standing back, watching the fight unfold with cold, calculating eyes. It was as if King Ardan was waiting for something—for the moment when Kael would fall.

But Kael wouldn't give him that satisfaction.

Elara stood beside him, her hands weaving through the air as she summoned her magic. Bolts of shimmering light shot from her fingertips, striking down the knights who dared come too close. But with each spell, Kael could see the strain on her face. The magic was taking its toll, especially after the encounter with Maelis.

"We can't hold them off forever," Kael said, slashing through another knight as he turned toward Elara. "We need to do something, or—"

Before he could finish, the ground beneath them shook violently, throwing both Kael and Elara off balance. The knights stumbled as well, their formation breaking apart as the earth trembled beneath their feet.

"What's happening?" Kael shouted over the roar of the shifting ground.

Elara's eyes widened in fear and understanding. "The ancient magic—it's reacting!"

A blinding light erupted from the monolith, shooting into the sky like a beacon. The runes on the stone glowed brighter than ever before, pulsating with raw, untamed energy. The air crackled with power, and Kael felt the magic pulling at him, drawing him toward the monolith.

And then, amid the chaos, a voice—a soft, childlike voice—echoed in the wind.

"Mother... Father..."

Kael froze, his heart skipping a beat. He turned toward Elara, who stood as still as a statue, her eyes wide with shock. "Did you hear that?" Kael asked, his voice barely audible.

Elara nodded, her hand resting on her stomach as if she could feel the voice coming from within her. "It's the child," she whispered, her voice filled with awe and disbelief. "Our child."

Before Kael could process what was happening, a figure began to materialize in front of the monolith, bathed in the glow of the ancient magic. At first, it was only a faint outline, but soon, the figure became clear—a young girl, no more than ten years old, with long, silvery hair and glowing violet eyes.

Kael's breath caught in his throat as he stared at the girl. There was no mistaking it. She was their child.

"Lyra," Elara whispered, her voice trembling with emotion.

The girl—Lyra—looked at them with eyes that held far more knowledge than her age should allow. "You've come to the crossroads," she said, her voice soft but powerful. "It's time to make a choice."

Kael stepped forward, his mind racing. "A choice? What do you mean?"

Lyra's gaze shifted between Kael and Elara, her expression unreadable. "The ancient magic can change the world, but it must be balanced. Light and dark, creation and destruction. If you wish to stop the war, you must decide which path to take."

Kael's heart pounded in his chest. This was the moment they had feared—the prophecy was coming true before their very eyes.

Their child, Lyra, stood at the center of it all, holding the power to either unite their worlds or tear them apart.

"But what will happen to you?" Elara asked, her voice filled with fear for their daughter.

Lyra's eyes softened as she looked at Elara. "I am a part of this magic, Mother. I was born from both worlds—witch and human, light and dark. My fate is tied to the balance of the magic."

Kael's fists clenched at his sides. "And what if we choose wrong? What if the magic destroys everything?"

Lyra's gaze met his, and for the first time, Kael saw a flicker of sadness in her eyes. "There is no wrong choice, Father. Only the choice you are willing to live with."

The ground shook again, and the monolith began to crack, the runes pulsing faster and faster. The ancient magic was reaching its peak, and they were running out of time.

Kael turned to Elara, his mind spinning. "What do we do?"

Elara's eyes were filled with tears, her hand trembling as she reached out to touch Lyra's cheek. "I don't know," she whispered, her voice breaking. "I don't know what's right anymore."

Lyra placed her small hand over Elara's, her touch gentle. "You do know, Mother. You've always known."

Elara closed her eyes, a single tear slipping down her cheek. She took a deep breath and turned to Kael. "We have to trust her," she said, her voice steady despite the tears. "We have to trust Lyra."

Kael's chest tightened, but he nodded, his heart swelling with a mixture of fear and hope. "We trust her."

Lyra smiled, the sadness in her eyes fading. "Then it's time."

She stepped forward, her small hand reaching out to touch the monolith. The moment her fingers brushed the stone, a shockwave of magic exploded from the monolith, sweeping across the plateau like a tidal wave. Kael felt the force of the magic wash over him, filling him with both light and darkness, hope and despair.

For a moment, the world seemed to stand still, suspended in the balance between two worlds.

And then, as suddenly as it had begun, the light faded, and the air grew still.

Kael blinked, his heart pounding as he looked around. The monolith stood silent, the runes no longer glowing. The ground was still, the wind calm. The battle had stopped, the knights and witches alike frozen in place, their weapons lowered as if the magic had drained the fight from them.

And in the center of it all stood Lyra, her violet eyes glowing softly. She turned to Kael and Elara, a serene smile on her face.

"The choice has been made," she said quietly.

Kael's breath caught in his throat. "What does that mean?"

Lyra stepped forward, her gaze filled with wisdom beyond her years. "The war is over. The magic has restored the balance between our worlds. But the cost..."

She looked down, her smile fading.

Kael's heart clenched. "Lyra, what cost?"

Lyra's voice was soft, almost a whisper. "I have to go. The magic that created me... it's time for me to return to it."

Elara let out a choked sob, reaching for her daughter. "No, Lyra, please..."

Lyra shook her head, her expression calm. "It's okay, Mother. This is how it's meant to be. You gave me life, and now I give it back to the world."

Kael felt his throat tighten, his heart breaking. "Lyra..."

Lyra looked up at him, her violet eyes filled with love. "Thank you, Father. For trusting me."

And with that, Lyra stepped into the monolith, her figure dissolving into light. The glow faded, leaving only silence in its wake.

Kael fell to his knees, his heart shattered as he stared at the place where his daughter had stood.

Elara collapsed beside him, her sobs breaking the silence as she clung to him, her body trembling with grief.

The war was over. The balance had been restored.

But their daughter was gone.

Arianna Reed

Chapter 12:
A Kingdom in Flames

Kael knelt beside the monolith, his body numb from the overwhelming grief that had overtaken him. His daughter—Lyra—was gone, her light extinguished just as quickly as it had appeared. He could still feel the remnants of the ancient magic lingering in the air, but it was a hollow echo compared to the presence of the vibrant, powerful child they had barely begun to know.

Elara's sobs filled the silence as she clung to Kael, her body trembling. Her heartache was mirrored in his, the weight of their loss almost too much to bear. Kael wrapped his arms around her, pulling her close, but no words came. Nothing could ease the pain of losing their child.

The wind that had howled through the mountains was now eerily still, as if the world itself had stopped to mourn. The knights, the witches—everyone who had come to this battlefield stood frozen, their weapons lowered, eyes wide with disbelief. For the first time, there was no fight left in them. The magic had drained them, just as it had taken Lyra from them.

King Ardan stood apart from the others, his face twisted in a mix of fury and confusion. He had come here to end the threat, to destroy the witch and reclaim his son, but the scene before him defied everything he had believed. His voice, sharp and commanding, cut through the stillness.

"Kael," Ardan growled, stepping forward. "What have you done?"

Kael lifted his head slowly, his eyes bloodshot and filled with rage. "What have I done?" he repeated, his voice low and shaking. "You still don't understand, do you?"

Ardan's gaze hardened. "I understand that you've been bewitched—manipulated by that witch's magic. Your child... she was never meant to exist."

Kael rose to his feet, his entire body trembling with anger. "She was meant to exist! And she sacrificed herself to save both our worlds!"

Ardan's face contorted with disgust. "You've become a fool, Kael. A traitor to your own bloodline."

Kael's fury boiled over, and he stepped toward his father, his fists clenched. "The only fool here is you, Father. You've been blinded by your hatred for so long that you can't even see the truth when it's right in front of you. Lyra saved us. She gave her life to end the war you've been so desperate to start."

Ardan sneered. "You think this is over? You think one sacrifice can undo centuries of conflict between humans and witches? You're more naive than I thought."

Kael felt his blood run cold at his father's words. Even now, after everything, Ardan was still clinging to his hatred. Kael had hoped that Lyra's sacrifice would be enough to change his father's heart, but it seemed that nothing could reach him.

Elara stepped forward, her face pale but determined. "This war is over, Ardan. Whether you accept it or not, the magic has restored the balance. If you continue to fight, you'll be fighting against the very forces that keep this world from falling apart."

Ardan turned his cold gaze on her, his lip curling with disdain. "You think you can lecture me about the balance of the world? You, a witch?"

Kael's heart pounded with fury. "This isn't about you or your hatred anymore, Father. It's about the future. The child you called an abomination saved your kingdom from destruction."

Ardan's face twisted with anger, but before he could respond, a loud rumble echoed through the mountains. The ground trembled once more, and Kael looked around in alarm.

"What now?" Kael muttered under his breath.

Suddenly, a figure emerged from the shadows—Rowen, one of Ardan's most trusted advisors. His face was grim, and his eyes filled with urgency as he approached the king.

"Your Majesty," Rowen said, his voice tight with concern. "There's been an attack."

Kael's heart skipped a beat. "An attack? Where?"

Rowen's expression darkened. "The capital. The witches... they've struck back."

Elara's eyes widened in shock. "No, that can't be. The coven wouldn't—"

"Wouldn't they?" Ardan interrupted, his voice thick with accusation. "This is their doing, Elara. This was their plan all along."

Kael felt a surge of dread as the reality of the situation sank in. The coven had acted, striking at the kingdom while they were distracted. But why? Had they sensed the magic shifting? Had they believed that Kael and Elara had failed?

"We need to go back," Kael said, his voice urgent. "We need to stop this before it gets worse."

Ardan's eyes flashed with triumph, his lips curling into a sneer. "So now you see, Kael? This war will never end. The witches will never stop until we've destroyed them."

Kael's jaw tightened. "I'll stop it, Father. But not your way. I'll stop it without more bloodshed."

Without waiting for a response, Kael turned to Elara. "We need to reach the capital before it's too late."

Elara nodded, though her face was etched with worry. "We'll need to move quickly. If the coven has already struck, they'll be prepared for retaliation."

Kael glanced at his father, who stood unmoving, his face a mask of cold resolve. There was no reasoning with him, no chance of convincing him to see things differently. Kael had to act on his own.

"We're leaving," Kael said, his voice steady. "With or without you."

Ardan's eyes narrowed, but he made no move to stop them. "Do what you will, Kael. But when you fail, don't expect mercy."

Kael didn't respond. He turned on his heel and began the descent from the plateau, Elara at his side. His heart raced with fear and anger, but he pushed it all aside. The capital was in danger, and they had to stop the fighting before everything was lost.

The journey back to the capital was a blur of frantic movement and growing dread. By the time Kael and Elara reached the outskirts of the city, the smell of smoke filled the air. Fires raged in the distance, casting a hellish glow over the city walls. The streets were filled with panicked citizens, fleeing the destruction as witches and soldiers clashed in a chaotic battle.

Kael's heart sank as he surveyed the devastation. This was exactly what they had been trying to prevent, and yet, it had come to pass.

"We have to find the coven," Elara said, her voice filled with urgency. "If we can convince them to stop—"

"Look!" Kael interrupted, pointing toward the city square.

A group of witches stood in the center of the square, their magic swirling around them as they fought off the advancing soldiers. At their head was Ayla, one of the younger witches from Elara's coven. Her face was a mask of determination, her hands crackling with raw power.

Elara's eyes widened in recognition. "Ayla..."

Without another word, Elara ran toward the square, Kael following close behind. As they neared the battle, Ayla caught sight of them, her eyes narrowing in surprise.

"Elara?" Ayla called out, her voice a mixture of shock and anger. "What are you doing here? You betrayed us!"

Elara shook her head, her voice desperate. "Ayla, stop! You don't understand! The ancient magic has been restored—the war is over!"

Ayla's face twisted with rage. "The war will never be over as long as they hunt us! We can't stop now. Not after everything!"

Kael stepped forward, his voice firm. "You don't have to fight anymore. Lyra—our daughter—sacrificed herself to bring peace between our worlds. Don't let her sacrifice be in vain."

Ayla hesitated, her expression torn. "Lyra... she's gone?"

Elara nodded, tears welling in her eyes. "She gave her life to end this. Please, Ayla, you have to stop."

Ayla's hands trembled, the magic flickering in her grasp. For a long moment, she seemed to consider their words. Then, slowly, she lowered her hands, the magic dissipating into the air.

The soldiers, seeing the witches' surrender, paused, their weapons still raised but no longer advancing.

Elara stepped forward, her voice soft but filled with determination. "It's over."

Kael let out a shaky breath as the tension in the air eased. The fighting had stopped—for now. But the wounds left by the war would take time to heal, and the road ahead was still uncertain.

The capital burned, but for the first time in years, there was hope for a new beginning.

The Heir of Two Worlds

Chapter 13: The Sorcerer's Return

The fires that had ravaged the capital still smoldered in the distance, casting an eerie orange glow over the ruined city. The smell of smoke and ash filled the air as Kael and Elara stood at the edge of the city square, watching as the last of the witches and soldiers began to retreat, their energy spent. The battle was over—for now.

Kael's heart ached with the weight of everything that had been lost. Lyra's sacrifice had stopped the immediate fighting, but the damage left behind by years of conflict would take far longer to heal. He turned to Elara, whose violet eyes were filled with both relief and sorrow.

"It's not enough," she whispered, her voice hoarse from the strain of battle. "We stopped this fight, but there will always be others. The magic we've awakened... it's too powerful. There are those who will seek to control it."

Kael's chest tightened. He knew she was right. The ancient magic that had surged through the monolith was now a part of the world again, and its influence could not be undone. They had stopped the immediate threat, but the danger wasn't over.

"What do we do?" Kael asked, his voice heavy with the uncertainty of their future.

Elara looked toward the horizon, her face filled with quiet determination. "We have to find the source of the corruption—the darkness that has tainted the ancient magic. If we don't, it will consume everything."

Kael nodded, though the thought of facing an even greater threat weighed heavily on him. They had already lost so much, and yet it seemed their journey was far from over.

Suddenly, a chill ran down Kael's spine. The air around them shifted, growing colder, and a strange, oppressive silence fell over the city square. Kael glanced at Elara, whose face had gone pale. She sensed it too—something dark was approaching.

Before either of them could react, a shadowy figure materialized at the far end of the square. The figure was cloaked in darkness, its face hidden beneath a hood that obscured its features. But even from a distance, Kael could feel the raw power emanating from the figure—a power far greater than anything they had faced before.

Elara's hand tightened around Kael's arm, her voice barely above a whisper. "It can't be..."

"Who is that?" Kael asked, his voice low and tense.

Elara swallowed hard, her eyes wide with fear. "It's the sorcerer. The one who was banished long ago. He's returned."

Kael's heart raced as he stared at the figure. The sorcerer—the one who had been whispered about in legends, a being of immense power who had once nearly destroyed both the kingdom and the coven. He had been exiled to the farthest reaches of the magical realm, never to return. But now, he stood before them, more powerful than ever.

The sorcerer stepped forward, his dark robes swirling around him like smoke. His voice, deep and cold, echoed across the square. "You thought you could awaken the ancient magic without consequences?"

Kael stepped in front of Elara, his sword already in hand. "What do you want?"

The sorcerer's laugh was low and menacing. "What I've always wanted. Power. Control over both worlds—yours and hers." His gaze shifted to Elara, his eyes gleaming with cruel intent. "You've unleashed the magic, and now it belongs to me."

Elara's breath hitched, her hands trembling as she summoned what little magic she had left. "We won't let you take it."

The sorcerer's smile widened. "You have no choice. You and your child were always part of the prophecy. But now the child is gone, and the balance has shifted in my favor."

Kael's blood ran cold at the mention of Lyra. His fists clenched in fury. "You will never control that magic," he growled, his voice filled with determination. "It doesn't belong to you."

The sorcerer tilted his head, as if considering Kael's words. "And what will you do to stop me, Prince? Your sword is useless against me."

Kael gritted his teeth, knowing the sorcerer was right. He had no magic of his own, no way to fight the overwhelming power that the sorcerer commanded. But he couldn't let this darkness consume everything they had fought for.

The Heir of Two Worlds

"We have to find a way," Kael whispered to Elara, his voice filled with desperation. "We can't let him take the magic."

Elara's eyes were filled with tears, her body trembling with exhaustion. "I don't know if I have the strength left, Kael. The magic... it's already slipping away from me."

The sorcerer raised his hand, and a surge of dark energy crackled through the air, spreading out like a web of shadowy tendrils. The ground beneath them began to crack, the buildings around them crumbling as the darkness spread.

Kael stepped forward, raising his sword even though he knew it wouldn't be enough. But before he could make a move, a voice—a soft, familiar voice—rang out through the darkness.

"Stop."

Kael's heart skipped a beat, and he turned, his breath catching in his throat.

There, standing at the edge of the square, was Lyra.

Kael's mind reeled with disbelief. Lyra—his daughter—was alive. Her silvery hair flowed in the wind, and her violet eyes glowed with the same power she had displayed before. But there was something different about her now—something ethereal, as if she was more spirit than flesh.

"Lyra?" Elara whispered, her voice filled with awe and confusion. "How...?"

Lyra stepped forward, her gaze fixed on the sorcerer. "You cannot have the magic," she said, her voice steady and filled with authority far beyond her years. "It belongs to no one."

The sorcerer's eyes flashed with anger. "You? You are nothing but a child—a failed prophecy. You cannot stand against me."

Lyra's expression didn't waver. "I am the balance. The magic flows through me, and I will protect it."

Kael's heart swelled with pride and fear as he watched his daughter face down the most powerful being they had ever encountered. He wanted to rush to her side, to protect her, but he knew this was beyond his ability. Lyra had become something far greater than either of them had imagined.

The sorcerer sneered, raising his hand to strike her down, but before he could unleash his power, Lyra lifted her own hand, and a brilliant light erupted from her palm. The darkness recoiled, hissing and crackling as the light surged toward the sorcerer, forcing him back.

"You cannot win," Lyra said, her voice calm and resolute. "The magic is beyond your control."

The sorcerer snarled in frustration, his dark power faltering under the force of Lyra's light. "This is not over," he spat, his voice filled with venom. "I will return, and when I do, I will take everything from you."

With a final wave of his hand, the sorcerer vanished into the shadows, disappearing as suddenly as he had appeared.

The square fell silent, the air heavy with the aftermath of the battle. Kael and Elara stared at Lyra, their hearts pounding with disbelief and relief.

"Lyra," Kael whispered, stepping forward. "How... how are you here?"

Lyra turned to face her parents, her eyes softening. "I was never truly gone, Father. The magic that created me—the balance—still exists. I'm a part of it now, and as long as the magic remains, so will I."

Tears filled Elara's eyes as she reached for her daughter, her voice trembling with emotion. "We thought we'd lost you."

Lyra smiled, her hand resting on Elara's cheek. "You'll never lose me. I'll always be with you."

Kael felt his throat tighten as he watched the reunion between mother and daughter. His heart swelled with gratitude and love, though a deep sadness lingered beneath the surface. Lyra was no longer the child they had known. She was something more—something greater than they could have imagined.

But she was still their daughter.

"What happens now?" Kael asked, his voice filled with uncertainty.

Lyra's gaze turned to the horizon, her expression thoughtful. "The world will heal. The magic will return to its rightful place, and the balance will be restored. But the fight isn't over. There are still those who will seek to control the magic, to twist it for their own gain."

Kael nodded, his heart heavy. "We'll protect it. We'll protect you."

Lyra's smile was bittersweet. "You won't need to protect me. I'll protect all of you."

And with that, Lyra's form began to fade, the light surrounding her growing brighter until she was nothing more than a glowing silhouette.

"I love you, Father. I love you, Mother," she said softly, her voice echoing through the air as she disappeared into the light.

Kael and Elara stood in silence, the empty square stretching out before them. The danger had passed, but the loss of their daughter still hung in the air, bittersweet and undeniable.

The world would heal, but the scars of their journey would remain.

Chapter 14:
The Prince's Sacrifice

Kael stood at the edge of the city, watching as the fires in the distance began to die down. The capital, once a symbol of his family's power and legacy, lay in ruins, scarred by the war between humans and witches. Despite the chaos that had consumed the kingdom, a strange, uneasy calm now settled over the land.

Beside him, Elara was silent, her eyes distant as she stared into the horizon. Lyra's final words still echoed in her mind, a reminder that their daughter, though no longer with them in physical form, would always be a part of the magic that bound their world together. But the loss of Lyra still weighed heavily on them both. There was no undoing the sacrifice she had made to protect the balance between their worlds.

Kael clenched his fists, a bitter taste in his mouth as he thought of what came next. The war might have ended, but the fractures between their people remained. The hatred, the distrust—it would take more than peace to heal those wounds. And worse, his father, King Ardan, would never forgive him for what had happened.

"He won't stop," Kael said quietly, breaking the silence. "My father will keep fighting, even after everything that's happened. He won't let this go."

Elara turned to face him, her violet eyes filled with sadness. "You're right," she said softly. "Ardan's hatred runs too deep. He'll never accept peace with the witches."

Kael's heart sank at her words. He had known this for a long time, but hearing it aloud made it all the more real. King Ardan's hatred for witches had driven every decision, every war, and Kael had been caught in the middle, torn between his loyalty to his family and his love for Elara.

"I don't know how to stop him," Kael admitted, his voice filled with frustration. "If I return to the kingdom, I'll be branded a traitor. If I stay away, the war will continue without me."

Elara placed a hand on his arm, her touch gentle. "There is a way," she said quietly. "But it will require a sacrifice."

Kael frowned, turning to her. "What do you mean?"

Elara's gaze was steady, though there was a hint of sorrow in her eyes. "You need to confront your father. Not as his son, but as a leader—a ruler. The people need to see that you're not just running away from him. You need to stand against him, for the sake of both our worlds."

Kael's heart pounded in his chest. Confront his father? The thought filled him with both fear and resolve. He had spent his entire life in Ardan's shadow, always expected to follow in his father's footsteps. But he had changed. His love for Elara, the bond they had formed, and the sacrifices they had made had shown him a different path. A path his father could never understand.

"And if he refuses to listen?" Kael asked, though he already knew the answer.

Elara's expression darkened. "Then you'll have to take the throne."

Kael's breath caught in his throat. Take the throne. The very idea felt like a betrayal, but at the same time, he knew Elara was right. His father's reign had brought nothing but destruction and hatred. If there was ever to be peace, real peace, Kael would have to take his place as king.

"It won't be easy," Elara continued, her voice steady. "Your father will see it as the ultimate betrayal, but you have the people's support. They've seen the destruction caused by this war. They've seen what you're willing to sacrifice to bring peace. You have to make them believe in a future without hatred."

Kael looked down, his mind spinning. Could he really do it? Could he challenge his father for the throne? It would mean turning his back on the man who had raised him, the man who had taught him everything he knew about ruling. But it would also mean saving the kingdom from further destruction, from a cycle of violence that would never end if Ardan remained in power.

"I don't know if I'm ready," Kael said softly.

Elara stepped closer, placing her hand on his cheek. "You are. You've been ready for this since the day you chose to love me, despite everything standing in our way. That was the first step. This is the next."

Kael closed his eyes, leaning into her touch. He wanted to believe her, wanted to believe that he was strong enough to face his father and lead the kingdom into a new era. But doubt gnawed at him. His father had always been a towering figure in his life, and the thought of challenging him felt like a battle he wasn't sure he could win.

But as he looked into Elara's eyes, he saw the faith she had in him. She believed in him. And if she could believe in him, then perhaps he could find the strength to believe in himself.

"I'll do it," Kael said, his voice firmer now. "I'll confront him."

Elara smiled, though there was a flicker of sadness in her gaze. "We'll do it together."

The next morning, Kael and Elara set out for the castle. The journey was filled with tension, both of them knowing what awaited them at the end. Kael's heart raced with every step, his mind replaying the countless confrontations he had with his father over the years. But this time, it wouldn't be a simple argument. This time, everything was on the line.

When they reached the castle gates, they were met by a group of guards. The captain stepped forward, his expression grim.

"Prince Kael," he said, his voice filled with uncertainty. "The king has been waiting for you."

Kael nodded, his jaw clenched. "I'm here to speak with him."

The captain hesitated, glancing at Elara. "And the witch?"

"She's with me," Kael said firmly. "She will always be with me."

The captain gave a curt nod, then stepped aside, allowing them to pass.

As they made their way through the castle, Kael's heart pounded in his chest. Every step felt heavier, the weight of what was about to happen pressing down on him. He glanced at Elara, whose face was calm but determined. She was his anchor, his strength. Together, they could face anything.

When they reached the throne room, the doors swung open, revealing King Ardan seated on his throne, his face twisted in a mixture of anger and contempt. The room was filled with nobles, soldiers, and advisors, all watching the confrontation with bated breath.

"Kael," Ardan said, his voice cold. "You've returned."

Kael stepped forward, his chin raised, his voice steady. "I've come to end this."

Ardan's eyes narrowed, his hand gripping the armrest of his throne. "End this? You think you have the power to end anything? You're a traitor to your own blood, consorting with a witch. You've thrown away your birthright."

Kael's fists clenched at his sides, but he kept his voice calm. "I haven't thrown away anything. I've chosen a different path—one that doesn't lead to endless war and destruction. You've ruled this kingdom with hatred and fear for too long, Father. It's time for that to end."

The room fell deathly silent as Kael's words hung in the air. The tension was palpable, and Kael could feel the eyes of everyone in the room on him. His father's gaze darkened, his expression filled with fury.

"You would dare challenge me?" Ardan hissed, rising from his throne. "You think you can take my place?"

Kael's heart raced, but he stood his ground. "Yes. For the sake of the kingdom. For the sake of peace."

Ardan's face twisted in rage, and he stepped toward Kael, his voice a low growl. "You are no son of mine."

Kael's chest tightened, but he didn't flinch. "Then I'll be king without you."

For a moment, it seemed as if Ardan would strike him down right then and there, but before he could move, Elara stepped forward, her voice steady. "It's over, Ardan. The people won't follow you anymore. They want peace, and they will follow Kael."

The king's eyes flashed with hatred as he turned to Elara. "You! This is all because of you—because of your witchcraft, your lies!"

Elara's gaze didn't waver. "This is because of your hatred, Ardan. Your unwillingness to see that we can live in peace."

Ardan's hand twitched, but before he could lash out, a voice rang out from the crowd.

"He's right," a nobleman said, stepping forward. "We've had enough of this war. The people want peace."

One by one, others began to speak, their voices rising in agreement.

Ardan's face paled, his eyes wide with disbelief. The support he had once commanded was crumbling before him, and for the first time, he realized that his reign was slipping through his fingers.

"You've lost," Kael said quietly. "It's time to let go."

Ardan's shoulders sagged, the weight of his defeat crashing down on him. He stared at Kael for a long moment, his face a mixture of anger and sorrow. Then, without a word, he turned and walked away, disappearing into the shadows of the throne room.

Kael let out a breath he hadn't realized he'd been holding, his entire body trembling with the weight of what had just happened.

It was over.

Chapter 15:
The Coven's Decision

The throne room was eerily silent in the wake of King Ardan's retreat. Kael stood at the center of the vast chamber, his heart still pounding from the confrontation. It was over—his father had relinquished his power, but the path ahead was uncertain. He could feel the weight of the kingdom pressing down on him, the expectations and fears of everyone in the room heavy in the air.

Elara stood beside him, her presence a source of strength and calm. She had been his guiding light through this dark and tumultuous journey, and now, with his father gone and the kingdom looking to him for leadership, Kael knew he couldn't do this alone.

The nobles and soldiers, who had watched the confrontation in tense silence, began to murmur among themselves, their voices filled with uncertainty and doubt. Kael's chest tightened as he looked around, wondering if they would accept him as their king—especially with Elara by his side. His father's hatred for witches had been deeply ingrained in the kingdom, and it would take more than a single confrontation to undo that damage.

Before Kael could speak, the doors to the throne room swung open, and a group of witches entered, led by Maelis, the leader of

Elara's coven. Their dark cloaks billowed behind them as they crossed the threshold, their faces stern and unreadable. Kael tensed at the sight of them, unsure of what this meant.

Elara's expression darkened as she recognized Maelis. "They've come for me," she whispered, her voice filled with dread.

Kael's heart raced. "What do you mean?"

Elara's gaze didn't leave Maelis as she spoke. "The coven has strict rules about consorting with humans, especially royalty. They see our union as a threat—one that could destabilize the balance between our worlds."

Kael's fists clenched at his sides. "But they know the war is over. Lyra—"

"They don't care," Elara said softly, cutting him off. "They see me as a traitor."

Maelis stepped forward, his piercing gaze sweeping over Kael before settling on Elara. "Elara," he said, his voice cold and formal. "You've defied the laws of the coven. You've chosen a path that endangers us all."

Elara met his gaze with quiet defiance. "I chose a path of peace. A path that ended the war. You can't deny that."

Maelis' eyes narrowed. "The war may be over, but the consequences of your actions are far from finished. The balance of magic has been disrupted. The ancient magic has been awakened, and now the world teeters on the brink of chaos."

Kael stepped forward, his voice firm. "We did what we had to do to stop the war. Lyra—our daughter—sacrificed herself to restore the balance. You can't hold that against Elara."

Maelis' gaze flickered with disdain as he regarded Kael. "You speak of things you do not understand, Prince. The magic that flows through your bloodline is tainted by human ambition. You are not one of us."

Kael's jaw tightened, but before he could respond, Elara placed a hand on his arm, silently asking him to let her speak.

"I know the coven sees me as a threat," Elara said, her voice steady. "But I haven't betrayed our people. I've fought to protect them, just as I've fought to protect the humans. We are bound together by the magic of this world, whether we like it or not. Continuing this divide will only lead to more suffering."

Maelis' expression remained stony. "Your words do not change the fact that you've broken the laws of the coven. You've consorted with a prince, a human who seeks to rule over us."

Kael's heart sank at the accusation. He could see the doubt in the eyes of the other witches, their fear and mistrust of him clear. Despite everything he and Elara had done, the deep-rooted animosity between their people still lingered, threatening to unravel the fragile peace they had worked so hard to achieve.

"I don't seek to rule over anyone," Kael said, his voice calm but firm. "I seek to unite our worlds. We've both suffered too much loss. The fighting, the hatred—it has to end."

Maelis turned his cold gaze back to Elara. "And you believe that uniting with him will bring peace?"

Elara hesitated for a moment, then nodded. "Yes. I do. Kael has proven that he is willing to fight for peace, even if it means standing against his own father. We've both sacrificed everything to bring an end to this war. But if the coven cannot accept that, then—"

She trailed off, her voice trembling slightly. Kael reached for her hand, squeezing it tightly, offering her his silent support.

Maelis' expression darkened, but he said nothing. The tension in the room was thick, the silence stretching on as everyone waited for his response.

Finally, one of the witches stepped forward—a younger woman named Ayla, whose eyes were filled with uncertainty. "Elara is right," Ayla said quietly. "We can't keep fighting forever. The magic that binds us all is the same, whether we are human or witch. If we continue to divide ourselves, we'll only destroy everything we've fought to protect."

Maelis shot her a sharp look, but Ayla didn't back down. Her words seemed to resonate with some of the other witches, who exchanged hesitant glances.

Kael's heart swelled with hope. Perhaps, finally, there was a chance to bridge the divide between their worlds.

But Maelis was not ready to concede. "You would throw away centuries of tradition, of protection, for the sake of an ideal that cannot be achieved?" he asked, his voice filled with cold disdain.

Ayla stepped forward, her chin raised. "The traditions we've held onto have caused nothing but pain and suffering. It's time for something new."

Maelis' face twisted with anger, but before he could respond, Elara spoke again. "I'm not asking you to abandon our ways," she said softly. "But we have to evolve. We have to find a way to live in peace with the humans. If we don't, the ancient magic will continue to wreak havoc on both our worlds. We've seen what it can do when it's out of balance."

The room fell silent again, the weight of Elara's words hanging in the air.

For a long, tense moment, no one spoke. Kael could feel the eyes of the entire court on him and Elara, waiting for Maelis' response.

Finally, Maelis let out a slow breath, his expression unreadable. "Very well," he said, his voice low and measured. "We will allow this—union. But know this, Elara: your path is one fraught with danger. The balance of magic is fragile, and should it ever be threatened again, we will act to protect our own."

Elara nodded, though Kael could see the sadness in her eyes. She knew, just as he did, that the road ahead would not be easy.

But it was a start.

Kael let out a breath he hadn't realized he was holding, relief flooding through him. They had succeeded—at least for now. The witches had agreed to peace, but the tension between their worlds still simmered beneath the surface, waiting for a moment to boil over.

As the witches began to leave the throne room, Maelis paused, his cold gaze locking onto Kael. "You may have won their favor today, Prince," he said quietly. "But don't think for a moment that we will ever trust you."

Kael met Maelis' gaze, his voice steady. "I'm not asking for your trust. I'm asking for peace."

Maelis said nothing more as he turned and left the room, his cloak billowing behind him.

When the last of the witches had gone, Kael turned to Elara, his heart pounding with a mixture of relief and exhaustion. "We did it," he whispered, pulling her into his arms.

Elara leaned into him, her body trembling with emotion. "We did," she said softly, though there was a sadness in her voice that Kael couldn't ignore.

He pulled back slightly, looking into her eyes. "What's wrong?"

Elara shook her head, her expression weary. "It's not over, Kael. There's still so much work to be done. The witches may have agreed to peace, but the distrust between our people runs deep. This is just the beginning."

Kael nodded, though his heart ached at the truth of her words. "We'll face it together. Whatever comes."

Elara smiled, though it was bittersweet. "Yes. Together."

Arianna Reed

Chapter 16:
A Fragile Peace

The days that followed the confrontation in the throne room were a whirlwind of change for the kingdom. Word spread quickly that King Ardan had stepped down, and Kael had taken the throne, not as a conqueror, but as a ruler seeking peace. The news brought both hope and uncertainty to the people, who had lived under the shadow of war for so long that many couldn't remember what peace felt like.

Kael sat in the newly restored council chamber, flanked by advisors—some loyal to his father and others who had begun to support his vision for a unified kingdom. Despite the air of civility, tension hung in the room like a heavy fog, unspoken but ever-present.

The advisors, many of them older men with deeply ingrained beliefs, watched him with guarded expressions. They had agreed to follow him, but Kael knew that trust would take time. And with Elara by his side, their suspicion was heightened.

"We have reports from the northern villages," Lord Rowen began, his voice dry and matter-of-fact. "They've been seeing strange activity—magical disturbances. Some believe the coven is behind it."

Kael frowned. "We've already made a truce with the coven. Why would they continue to stir unrest?"

Rowen exchanged a glance with Lord Harwin, one of the elder councilors who had long supported King Ardan's policies. "Not all witches answer to Maelis and his coven," Harwin said. "There are other rogue factions—witches who don't respect your peace or the coven's authority."

Kael's heart sank at the news. The rogue witches had always been a problem, operating in the shadows, independent of the coven's control. They were wild and unpredictable, driven by their own desires, often feeding into the fears that humans had long harbored about magic.

"What do we do about them?" Kael asked, his voice tense.

Rowen cleared his throat. "Your father would have dealt with them swiftly—sent troops to root them out before they became a threat. I suggest you do the same."

Kael bristled at the mention of his father's methods. The old way—violence, suppression—was exactly what had fueled the division between humans and witches. But he couldn't ignore the problem either. The rogue witches posed a real threat, not just to the kingdom, but to the fragile peace they had worked so hard to establish.

"We need to handle this carefully," Kael said, his voice firm. "We can't afford to start another conflict. I'll send envoys to the coven to see if they can help bring these rogue witches under control."

Harwin raised an eyebrow. "You trust the coven to police their own?"

Kael glanced at Elara, who sat quietly beside him, her face calm but alert. She had been through more than anyone in the room could understand, and her connection to both worlds made her insight invaluable.

"We have to," Kael said, his tone brooking no argument. "We can't handle this the way my father would have. That path only leads to more war."

The room fell silent, the advisors exchanging uneasy glances. Kael could feel the tension building, the unspoken doubts swirling around him like a storm. He had taken the throne with a promise of peace, but the challenges of ruling a divided kingdom were far greater than he had anticipated.

"Very well, Your Majesty," Rowen said at last, though his tone was cautious. "We'll proceed with your plan for now. But if these rogue witches become a danger to the kingdom, we'll need to act swiftly."

Kael nodded, though the weight of the decision pressed down on him. He was trying to build a new future, one that didn't rely on fear and hatred. But that future felt fragile—one misstep, and everything could fall apart.

Later that evening, Kael and Elara walked through the castle gardens, the cool night air a welcome relief from the suffocating tension of the council chamber. The stars glittered above them, and the moon cast a soft glow over the flowers and winding paths.

Kael's mind was heavy with the decisions he had made that day, but Elara's presence beside him brought a sense of calm. They had been through so much together, and now, more than ever, he needed her by his side.

"I can feel your worry," Elara said softly, her hand slipping into his. "You're carrying so much, Kael."

Kael sighed, squeezing her hand gently. "I just don't know if I'm doing the right thing. Every decision feels like it could lead to disaster."

Elara stopped walking, turning to face him. "You're doing what no one else has had the courage to do. You're trying to break the cycle of hatred. That's not an easy path, but it's the right one."

Kael looked into her violet eyes, his heart swelling with love and gratitude. "I couldn't do this without you. You keep me grounded when everything else feels like it's slipping away."

Elara smiled, though there was a flicker of sadness in her gaze. "We're in this together, Kael. But there are forces at work that we don't fully understand yet. The rogue witches, the ancient magic... I fear that the peace we've fought for is more fragile than we realize."

Kael's stomach churned with unease. He had sensed the same thing—the balance between their worlds was still precarious, and any small disruption could tip it toward chaos. "What do we do?" he asked quietly.

Elara's eyes darkened with thought. "We need to be ready. The rogue witches won't listen to reason, and if they gain control of the ancient magic, they could unleash something far worse than we've seen before. We need allies—people who believe in this peace as much as we do."

Kael nodded, though the prospect of gathering allies felt daunting. His father's rule had left deep scars, and there were many who still viewed the witches as enemies. Winning their trust would take time—time they might not have.

"We'll start tomorrow," Kael said, determination filling his voice. "We'll reach out to the villages, the towns, and the people who have suffered because of this war. We'll show them that there's a better way."

Elara's smile returned, though it was tinged with the weight of what lay ahead. "I'll stand with you, always."

Kael pulled her close, pressing a soft kiss to her forehead. In that moment, despite the uncertainty and the challenges that awaited them, he felt a flicker of hope. They had come so far, and together, they could face whatever came next.

The next morning, Kael and Elara prepared to leave for the northern villages, where the reports of rogue witch activity had come from. They would travel with a small group of trusted soldiers and diplomats, hoping to avoid any further conflict and instead open a dialogue.

But as they made their final preparations, a messenger arrived at the castle, his face pale with fear.

"Your Majesty," the messenger said breathlessly, bowing low before Kael. "There's been an attack in the northern region. One of the villages has been completely destroyed."

Kael's heart sank, dread tightening in his chest. "Who was responsible?"

The messenger hesitated, then spoke the words Kael had feared. "The rogue witches, sire. They used dark magic to raze the village to the ground. There were no survivors."

Elara gasped, her hand flying to her mouth. Kael's mind raced, the horror of the news hitting him like a physical blow.

"This changes everything," Kael whispered, his voice filled with anguish.

Elara's eyes darkened with fear. "The peace we've worked for... it's slipping away."

Kael turned to the messenger, his heart pounding. "Ready the horses. We leave immediately."

As the messenger hurried away, Kael glanced at Elara, his voice grim. "We have to stop this before it gets worse."

Elara nodded, her face pale but determined. "We will. But we're running out of time."

The Heir of Two Worlds

Chapter 17:
The Gathering of Strength

Kael and Elara rode in silence as they left the sanctuary of the coven behind. The forest closed around them once more, the path ahead uncertain. Though they had secured Maelis' reluctant support, there was a lingering tension that wouldn't be dispelled so easily. The sacrifices and struggles still lay painfully fresh in their minds—a reminder of everything they had lost on the path to this fragile peace.

Elara glanced at Kael, her expression thoughtful. "Getting Maelis' help was a victory, but we need more allies. This fight isn't just about magic—it's about the whole kingdom. If we're going to face the rogue witches, we need to unite both humans and witches in this cause."

Kael nodded, determination etched into his features. "We need to show them that this isn't just a struggle for survival. It's an opportunity to build something new." The idea of unity seemed a distant dream, but their journey had taught them that hope could be found in the most unexpected places.

As they pushed forward through the forest, their senses remained alert. Tensions ran high on this critical mission, and every snap of a twig or rustle of leaves heightened their awareness. The soldiers accompanying them were experienced and loyal, but

Kael couldn't shake the feeling that something sinister lurked in the depths of the forest, watching their every move.

Night fell swiftly, enveloping them in its embrace, and Kael ordered the group to set up camp in a small clearing. The flickering flames of the campfire cast long shadows, illuminating weary faces and eyes glinting with resolve.

Sitting by the fire, Kael stared into the dancing flames, lost in thought. "We've risked everything to get this far," he began quietly, drawing the attention of the gathered soldiers and Elara. "We've faced impossible odds and will no doubt face them again tomorrow. Each of us knows what we're fighting for—for our lost villages, for peace, for a future where we're not defined by hate."

His words carried across the clearing, grounding their resolve. Each person present had felt the sting of loss in some form, and the collective yearning for a brighter tomorrow burned brightly within their hearts.

Elara reached out and placed a reassuring hand on Kael's shoulder, her gaze unwavering. "We need to find others who share our vision. There are villages untouched by the darkness, people who are willing to fight for this future as much as we are. We have to give them the chance to stand with us."

Kael's heart swelled with admiration for her unyielding spirit. "We'll find them," he promised, feeling the weight of their united purpose wrap around him like a shield. "For Lynmor, for us—and for Lyra."

In that moment, amongst the determined faces gathered around the fire, Kael sensed a flicker of unity—the kind of camaraderie he and Elara had fought to foster. The road ahead might be treacherous, but for now, they had each other. And in this fragile, destined alliance, perhaps they would forge the path to redemption.

Chapter 18:
The Gathering Storm

The coven's sanctuary buzzed with activity as witches prepared for the coming battle against the rogue witches. The air was thick with magic, swirling in unseen currents, as Kael and Elara stood with Maelis, discussing their next steps. Despite the tension between them, Kael could sense the gravity of the situation had softened the hard lines of Maelis' stance. He knew what was at stake.

"You'll need to be careful," Maelis said, his voice cold but steady as he addressed both Kael and Elara. "The rogue witches won't be easily found, but they will come to you if you draw them out. They've tasted power, and they won't stop until they control the ancient magic."

Kael nodded, his mind racing as he tried to formulate a plan. "How do we draw them out without endangering more people? We can't afford another massacre like the one in the northern village."

Maelis narrowed his eyes, his gaze thoughtful. "The rogue witches will be drawn to places where the magic is strongest. There are ancient sites—places of power hidden throughout the land. If you can reach one of these sites, they will come for the magic."

Elara's eyes widened slightly. "But that's dangerous. If we bring them to a place of power, they could tap into it before we even have a chance to stop them."

Maelis tilted his head. "It's a risk, yes. But you don't have many options. The longer we wait, the stronger they'll become. They're already using dark magic, and if they find one of these sites without interference, they could unleash forces that even we cannot control."

Kael's heart sank at the thought. It felt like they were walking into a trap—one they had no choice but to set themselves.

"Where's the closest site?" Kael asked, his voice firm.

Maelis gestured to a map laid out before them. "There's a place deep in the southern woods, near the border of the kingdom. It's a well of ancient magic, a place where the veil between worlds is thin. The rogue witches will sense it if you go there."

Kael studied the map, his jaw clenched. "And once they come, how do we stop them?"

Maelis' expression darkened. "That will depend on you and Elara. The coven will assist, but you will need to be ready. The rogue witches won't be easy to defeat. They're no longer bound by the laws of magic as we are. They'll fight without mercy."

Kael's chest tightened at the thought of facing such a powerful enemy. But he couldn't allow fear to hold him back. Too much was at stake.

"We'll go," Kael said, determination filling his voice. "We'll go to the southern woods and draw them out."

Elara's hand slipped into his, and though her eyes were filled with concern, she nodded. "I'll be with you, Kael. We'll face them together."

Maelis inclined his head, though there was no warmth in his gaze. "Very well. I'll send a few witches with you to assist. But remember, this battle is yours to fight. The coven cannot do everything for you."

Kael nodded, understanding the weight of Maelis' words. This was his responsibility now—not just as a prince, but as a leader. If they failed, it wouldn't just be the kingdom that suffered; it would be both their worlds.

The journey to the southern woods was tense, the air around them heavy with the feeling of impending danger. Kael and Elara rode in silence for most of the way, the weight of their mission pressing down on them. A small group of witches from the coven accompanied them, their faces somber and determined, but there was an unspoken fear that lingered between them.

As they neared the southern woods, the landscape began to change. The trees grew taller, their twisted branches casting long shadows over the forest floor. The air was thick with the scent of moss and damp earth, and the further they went, the more oppressive the atmosphere became.

"This place feels... wrong," Kael said, glancing around as the path narrowed.

Elara nodded, her violet eyes scanning the woods. "It's the magic. It's too strong here—it's almost overwhelming."

Kael could feel it too. The magic in this part of the world was different—ancient, wild, and unpredictable. It thrummed beneath the surface, like a current waiting to be unleashed.

"We need to be careful," Elara whispered. "The rogue witches will sense this place. They'll come for the power, but they'll also be able to draw strength from it."

Kael's heart pounded in his chest, his hand gripping the hilt of his sword. They were walking into a dangerous situation, but they had no other choice. They had to stop the rogue witches before they gained control of the ancient magic.

As they reached the heart of the woods, the clearing opened up before them. In the center stood a large stone structure—weathered and ancient, covered in glowing runes that pulsed with a soft, eerie light. It was a well of magic, just as Maelis had described—a place where the boundaries between their world and the magical realm were thin.

"This is it," Elara said softly, her voice barely a whisper. "We're here."

Kael dismounted, his heart racing as he looked around the clearing. The air felt charged, as if the very ground beneath their feet was alive with energy. They had to be ready—the rogue witches could arrive at any moment.

The witches from the coven began to form a protective circle around the stone structure, their hands raised as they chanted softly, weaving a barrier of magic around the well. Kael and Elara stood in the center, their eyes scanning the dark forest around them, waiting for the enemy to arrive.

For a long, tense moment, there was nothing but silence—the eerie stillness of the woods broken only by the faint hum of magic in the air. Kael's grip tightened on his sword, his muscles tensing as he prepared for the inevitable.

And then, without warning, the shadows began to move.

Kael's heart leapt into his throat as dark figures emerged from the trees, their forms wreathed in shadow and smoke. The rogue witches had arrived.

Their leader, a tall woman with wild, fiery hair and eyes that burned with a malevolent light, stepped forward, her voice cold and mocking. "You think you can stop us, Prince?" she sneered, her gaze shifting to Elara. "You and your witch have no idea what you've stepped into."

Kael raised his sword, his voice steady despite the fear gnawing at him. "We won't let you take this magic."

The rogue witch laughed, a harsh, grating sound. "This magic belongs to us. We've earned it. You don't understand the power you're trying to keep from us."

Elara stepped forward, her hands glowing with magic as she prepared for the coming fight. "We understand enough. You're destroying everything in your path for the sake of power. This isn't about balance—it's about greed."

The rogue witch's eyes narrowed, and with a flick of her hand, she unleashed a bolt of dark magic toward Elara.

Kael reacted instantly, raising his sword to block the attack, the force of the blow sending a shockwave through the clearing. The witches from the coven raised their hands, summoning shields of light to protect the well of magic as the battle erupted around them.

The rogue witches moved like shadows, their magic dark and twisted, striking out at Kael and Elara with deadly precision. Kael fought with everything he had, his sword cutting through the air as he deflected blow after blow, but the rogue witches were relentless.

Elara stood beside him, her magic crackling with power as she cast spell after spell, pushing the rogue witches back. But Kael could see the strain in her eyes—the toll the battle was taking on her.

"We can't hold them off forever," Elara shouted over the roar of magic.

Kael's heart pounded as he looked around the clearing, searching for any sign of hope. The rogue witches were growing stronger, their magic feeding off the power of the ancient well. If they didn't stop them soon, it would be too late.

Suddenly, a brilliant light erupted from the well of magic, blinding everyone in the clearing. Kael shielded his eyes, his heart racing as he felt the ground tremble beneath his feet.

When the light faded, Kael lowered his hand, his breath catching in his throat.

Standing at the center of the well, bathed in the glow of the ancient magic, was Lyra.

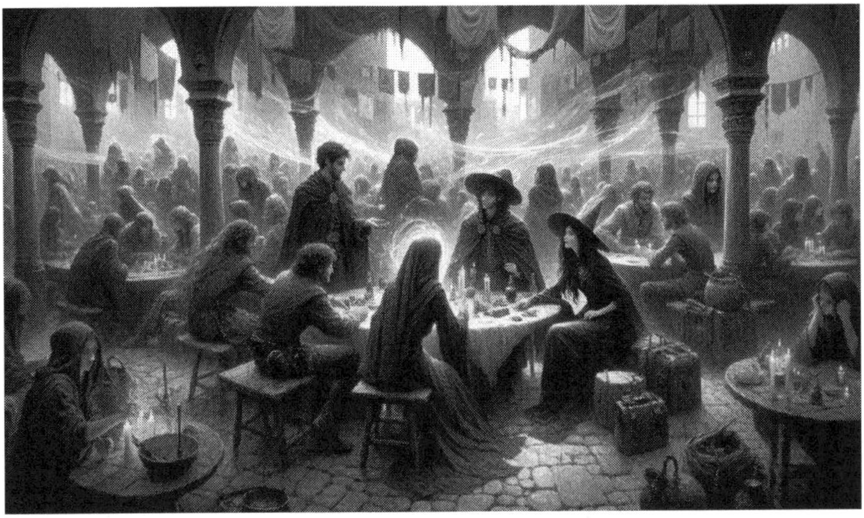

Chapter 19: Lyra's Power

The clearing was bathed in an ethereal light as Lyra stood in the center of the well of magic, her form glowing with a brilliant, almost otherworldly radiance. Kael's breath caught in his throat as he stared at his daughter—his heart racing with a mixture of awe, confusion, and hope. How was this possible? Lyra had sacrificed herself to restore balance, yet here she was, standing before them, more powerful than ever.

The rogue witches froze in their tracks, their eyes wide with shock as they gazed upon the child they had once believed gone. Even their leader, the fiery-haired witch, took a step back, her malevolent gaze flickering with uncertainty.

"Impossible," the rogue witch hissed, her voice trembling with disbelief. "You're supposed to be dead."

Lyra's violet eyes glowed with a quiet, steady power as she stepped forward, her voice calm but filled with authority. "I was never truly gone. I am the balance. And I won't allow you to take this magic."

Kael could barely contain his emotions as he watched Lyra. She had become something far more than just their daughter—something beyond human or witch. The ancient magic flowed through her, and she stood as a guardian of both worlds, protecting the fragile equilibrium that held them together.

Elara, standing beside Kael, took a step forward, her voice filled with emotion. "Lyra... how are you here?"

Lyra turned to her mother, her expression softening. "The magic that created me is eternal, Mother. It flows through me, just as it flows through this world. I've returned because the balance is once again threatened."

The rogue witch snarled, her hands crackling with dark energy. "You're just a child. You don't understand the power you're meddling with!"

Lyra's eyes glowed brighter, and with a wave of her hand, the dark magic surrounding the rogue witch dissipated like smoke in the wind. "I understand more than you ever will," Lyra said, her voice unwavering. "This power doesn't belong to you. It belongs to everyone."

Kael's heart swelled with pride and awe as he watched his daughter stand against the rogue witches. Her strength, her resolve—it was more than he had ever imagined. But even as hope flickered within him, he knew the fight wasn't over. The rogue witches wouldn't give up so easily.

"Stand down," Kael called out to the rogue witches, his voice firm. "This is your last chance. Leave now, or face the consequences."

The fiery-haired rogue witch's face twisted with rage as she raised her hands, summoning a swirling vortex of dark energy. "I won't be defeated by a child and a prince!" she shrieked, her voice filled with fury. "The ancient magic is ours!"

Arianna Reed

With a scream, she unleashed the full force of her dark magic toward Lyra, the energy crackling through the air like a storm of shadows.

But before the magic could reach her, Lyra raised her hand, and a shield of pure light erupted around her, absorbing the attack effortlessly. The dark energy fizzled out, leaving the rogue witch panting and drained, her power no match for Lyra's.

"You don't understand," Lyra said softly, her voice filled with sadness. "The more you try to take the magic, the more you destroy yourself."

The rogue witch stumbled backward, her eyes wild with desperation. "No... this can't be..."

Lyra stepped forward, her hand outstretched. "You can still choose. Let go of the darkness. There's still a way to make peace."

For a moment, the rogue witch hesitated, her face contorted with conflicting emotions. But then, with a snarl, she turned on her heel and fled into the forest, disappearing into the shadows. The other rogue witches followed her, their dark forms vanishing into the night.

Kael let out a breath he hadn't realized he'd been holding, his body trembling with the adrenaline of the fight. The danger had passed—for now. But as he looked at Lyra, standing in the center of the well of magic, he knew that this was only the beginning.

Lyra turned to her parents, her glowing form softening as the tension in the air eased. "It's over, for now. But they'll come back."

Elara rushed to Lyra's side, wrapping her arms around her daughter, tears streaming down her face. "You saved us," she whispered, her voice thick with emotion. "You've done so much..."

Lyra rested her head against her mother's shoulder, her voice gentle. "I'm only doing what I was meant to do, Mother. The magic is my responsibility now."

Kael stepped forward, his heart filled with a mixture of pride and sadness. "Lyra," he said softly, his voice trembling. "What happens next?"

Lyra pulled away from Elara and looked at her father, her violet eyes filled with a quiet, ancient wisdom. "I have to stay here, Father. The well of magic needs to be protected, and I'm the only one who can keep it balanced."

Kael's throat tightened, his heart aching at the thought of losing her again. "You're staying here? In the well?"

Lyra nodded, her voice soft but resolute. "It's where I belong now. The balance is fragile, and if the rogue witches—or anyone else—tries to disrupt it again, I have to be here to stop them."

Elara's hand tightened around Lyra's. "But you're still our daughter," she whispered, her voice breaking. "We've already lost you once..."

Lyra smiled, her eyes filled with love. "You'll never lose me, Mother. I'm a part of both worlds now, just like you and Father. And I'll always be with you."

Kael's heart broke as he realized the truth of her words. Lyra had become more than just their daughter—she was a guardian of the magic that flowed through their world, a being of immense power and responsibility. But she was still their child, and the thought of leaving her behind filled him with an indescribable sorrow.

"I'm so proud of you," Kael said, his voice thick with emotion. "You've done more than anyone could ever ask of you."

Lyra's smile softened, and she stepped forward, wrapping her arms around both her parents. "And I'm proud of you, too. You've both shown me what it means to protect the world we live in. Now it's my turn."

Kael and Elara held their daughter close, the weight of their shared love and sacrifice pressing down on them. They had fought for peace, and now, it was up to Lyra to protect the magic that held their worlds together.

As the night deepened and the clearing fell into a quiet calm, Kael knew that their journey was far from over. The rogue witches were still out there, and the balance of magic would always be at risk. But for the first time in a long time, Kael felt a sense of hope—a belief that they could build a future where humans and witches could live in harmony.

"We'll visit you," Elara whispered, her voice filled with love and sadness. "Every chance we get."

Lyra smiled, her glowing form fading slightly as she stepped back into the center of the well. "I'll be here."

As Kael and Elara watched their daughter return to her place of power, the light surrounding her dimmed, leaving the clearing bathed in the soft glow of the ancient magic.

Kael took Elara's hand, his heart heavy but filled with resolve. "We'll keep fighting for peace," he said quietly. "For her. For everyone."

Elara nodded, her eyes shimmering with unshed tears. "Yes. We will."

Together, they turned and began their journey back to the kingdom, leaving Lyra to watch over the well of magic. The battle was over, but the work of building a new world had only just begun.

Chapter 20: A New Beginning

Weeks had passed since the battle in the southern woods, and the kingdom was slowly beginning to heal. The rogue witches had scattered, their plans to seize the ancient magic thwarted by Lyra's power. Word of what had happened spread throughout the land, and while some still harbored fear and distrust, others began to believe in the possibility of peace—a peace that Kael and Elara had fought so hard to secure.

Kael stood on the balcony of the royal palace, gazing out over the city below. The morning sun bathed the capital in a golden light, casting long shadows across the streets and towers. The damage from the years of war was still visible—scars on buildings, empty spaces where families once lived—but there was also a sense of renewal. The people were rebuilding, and with each stone laid, hope was slowly returning.

Elara joined him on the balcony, her presence warm and comforting. She slipped her hand into his, and for a moment, they stood in silence, taking in the sight of their kingdom slowly coming back to life.

"How are you feeling?" Elara asked softly, her violet eyes filled with concern.

Kael sighed, his shoulders heavy with the weight of everything that had happened. "I'm not sure," he admitted. "I still feel like we're walking on fragile ground. The peace we've built... it could fall apart so easily."

Elara leaned into him, resting her head on his shoulder. "It's fragile, yes. But it's real. And it's worth fighting for."

Kael turned to look at her, his heart swelling with love and gratitude. "You've always believed in that, haven't you? Even when things seemed impossible."

Elara smiled softly. "Because I know what's at stake. I know what we're fighting for—for a world where our daughter doesn't have to protect us from ourselves. A world where humans and witches can live together, without fear."

Kael's chest tightened at the mention of Lyra. She was still at the well of magic, watching over the balance that held their worlds together. They had visited her a few times since the battle, but it wasn't the same as having her with them. She had taken on a responsibility far greater than any child should, and while Kael was proud of her, he couldn't help but feel the ache of her absence.

"She's stronger than any of us," Kael said quietly, his voice filled with a mixture of pride and sadness. "Stronger than I'll ever be."

Elara's smile softened. "She learned that from you."

Kael shook his head, a faint smile tugging at the corner of his lips. "I think she learned it from both of us."

They stood in silence for a while longer, the sounds of the city below drifting up to them—people working, children laughing, the hum of life continuing despite the challenges they had faced. It was a fragile peace, but it was a beginning.

"I've been thinking," Kael said after a moment, his voice contemplative. "About what comes next."

Elara glanced at him, curiosity in her eyes. "What do you mean?"

Kael sighed, running a hand through his hair. "We've been so focused on ending the war and stopping the rogue witches that we haven't had a chance to think about the future. About what kind of world we're trying to build."

Elara nodded thoughtfully. "You're right. The war may be over, but there's so much more to be done. We need to rebuild trust between humans and witches, to show people that we can live together without fear."

Kael's gaze drifted back to the city below. "And we need to make sure that the ancient magic stays balanced. That no one else tries to use it for their own gain."

Elara's expression grew serious. "That will be a challenge. There will always be those who seek power, who want to control what they don't understand."

Kael nodded, the weight of the task ahead pressing down on him. "I know. But we have to try. For Lyra. For everyone."

Elara's hand tightened around his, her voice soft but firm. "We will."

In the months that followed, Kael and Elara worked tirelessly to rebuild the kingdom. They traveled to every corner of the realm, speaking with the people, listening to their concerns, and working to heal the wounds left by the war. Slowly but surely, the divide between humans and witches began to narrow, though it was a long and difficult process.

Kael established new laws, ensuring that witches and humans had equal rights and protections under the crown. It wasn't easy—there were those who resisted the changes, who still clung to the old ways of fear and division—but Kael's resolve never wavered. He had seen the destruction that hatred could cause, and he refused to let it take root again.

Elara, too, played a vital role in shaping the new future. As both a witch and Kael's queen, she bridged the gap between their worlds, helping to foster understanding and cooperation. Her magic, once feared by many, became a symbol of hope and balance, a reminder that power could be used for good when wielded with wisdom and compassion.

Together, they forged a new path for the kingdom—one that was not built on fear or conquest, but on unity and peace.

One evening, several months after the battle in the southern woods, Kael and Elara made the journey back to the well of magic to visit Lyra. The southern woods were peaceful, the air filled with the soft rustle of leaves and the distant call of birds. It was a place that had once been filled with danger, but now, it felt like a sanctuary—a place where the world's magic was protected by their daughter.

When they reached the clearing, Lyra was waiting for them, her form bathed in the soft glow of the well's magic. She smiled as they approached, her eyes filled with love and warmth.

"Father, Mother," Lyra said softly, her voice filled with the wisdom of someone far beyond her years. "You've done so much."

Kael knelt beside his daughter, his heart swelling with pride. "We've done what we could. But it's you who has kept the balance, Lyra. You've protected us all."

Lyra's smile was gentle. "We've all played our part. The balance is something we all share."

Elara knelt beside them, her hand resting on Lyra's cheek. "We miss you," she whispered, her voice thick with emotion. "Every day."

Lyra leaned into her mother's touch, her eyes softening. "I'm always with you, even when I'm here."

Kael felt a lump rise in his throat as he looked at his daughter—his beautiful, strong daughter, who had become the guardian of their world. She was more than he had ever dreamed she could be, and yet, she was still the child he loved more than anything.

"You've made us so proud," Kael said, his voice trembling. "More than you'll ever know."

Lyra smiled, her eyes filled with love. "And I'm proud of you, too. Both of you."

They stayed with her for a while longer, talking about the kingdom, the people they had met, and the progress they had made. There was still much work to be done, but for the first time in a long time, Kael felt a sense of peace. The war was over, and though the future was uncertain, they were building something better—something worth fighting for.

As the sun began to set, casting the clearing in a golden light, Kael and Elara said their goodbyes, promising to return soon. Lyra watched them go, her glowing form a beacon of hope in the heart of the ancient woods.

And as they made their way back to the kingdom, hand in hand, Kael knew that they had finally found what they had been searching for all along—a new beginning.

Made in the USA
Middletown, DE
17 October 2024